SHOOTIN' MAN

BRADFORD SCOTT

SAGEBRUSH
Large Print Westerns

First published in the United States by Pyramid Books

First Isis Edition
published 2021
by arrangement with
Golden West Literary Agency

A catalogue record for this book is available
from the British Library.

ISBN 978–1–78541–869–3

Published by
Ulverscroft Limited
Anstey, Leicestershire

Set by Words & Graphics Ltd.
Anstey, Leicestershire
Printed and bound in Great Britain by
T J Books Ltd., Padstow, Cornwall

This book is printed on acid-free paper

CHAPTER
ONE

Mexican Pete's *cantina* crouched on the Palma water — front like a bloated frog in a bad temper. Its two big windows in warped frames seemed to bulge slightly, like a frog's eyes, and the wide entrance with swinging doors was not unlike a toad's underslung pouting mouth. Behind the garish false-front the low building swelled out on either side, with an uneven bowing to the timbers, and narrowed crookedly in the rear.

The saloon was, in fact, more than on the waterfront. Part of the structure was actually over it. In the dingy back rooms the swish and gurgle of water could be heard under the crooked and knot-holed floor boards. Through the holes seeped a dank breath smelling of salt and rotting seaweed.

Some of the floor boards were loose and, folks declared, could have told grim tales if given voice. But loose talking was not a feature of Mexican Pete's establishment.

Mexican Pete was tall, dark and astonishingly handsome. If he had any other name, nobody in Palma had ever heard it. His eyes, in startling contrast to his complexion, were light blue-gray, very clear, very keen and very masterful. He had a soft voice and a hard mouth. His hands were slender and finely shaped, and singularly adept with revolver, knife or deck of cards. He could do almost anything with those slender hands, even to keeping them perfectly still. He had a musical laugh that rang forth unexpectedly like a silver blade of sound.

The more respectable citizens of Palma did not care much for Pete himself, although nobody had ever been able to pin anything off-color on him. Lafe Secrets, who owned the big Dollar Saloon on Main Street and the paralleling big Forked S cattle ranch, usually a mild spoken man who got along well with his fellows, once said in a moment of irritation that the Gallo Rojo, as Pete called his place, should be burned to the ground and Pete along with it.

There were other buildings along the waterfront which housed saloons, gambling and dance halls and places the least said of the better — ramshackle structures that shouldered each other bad-temperedly — but the Gallo Rojo was outstanding, both in size and the nature of its habitues.

Strange men came to the Gallo Rojo. There were deep-water sailors from all parts of the world, who sailed into Palma on the little coastwise vessels that carried varied cargoes, not all of which showed on the manifest. There were lean, swarthy Mexicans from south of the Rio Grande, for Palma squatted on the coast within long riding distance from where the turgid flood of the stately River of the Palms stains the blue waters of the Gulf. There were lithe cowboys from the spreads to the east and north, and tight-lipped riders who drifted in from the desolate hills and marshlands to the west and the desert still farther west, their exact place of departure and destination unknown and not talked about. Quite a few of these last were "breeds" of one sort or another, usually with most of the vices and few of the virtues of the races they represented.

Yes, hard and unusual men came to Mexican Pete's Gallo Rojo, and evoked little comment.

But even the pay-night crowd at Mexican Pete's gave a second glance to the stranger who entered with the wind of a roaring Gulf storm at his back and raindrops glittering like jewels on the long slicker he quietly unbuttoned and hung on a peg near the end of the bar.

More than six feet in height, he was wide of shoulder, narrow of waist and hip, with arms that were long for even so tall a man. He had a hawk nose, long, level gray eyes with a dancing light of mocking laughter in their depths, hair so black that a blue shadow seemed to lie upon it, high cheek bones and a prominent jaw partially hidden by a stubble of short and thick beard, the kind of a beard which flourishes on long days in the saddle and many of them.

The newcomer's mouth was rather wide, with an upward quirking at the corners that somewhat relieved the tinge of fierceness evinced by the prominent nose and powerful jaw.

He wore the careless, efficient garb of the rangeland in such a way that it seemed a very part of the man and gave to one familiar with such things an impression of knightly armor. An integral part of the man, too, were the heavy black guns suspended in carefully worked and oiled cut-out holsters that swung from double cartridge belts encircling his lean waist.

At the moment, Ranger Walt Slade looked to perfection the part of a chuck-line riding cowhand who had recently known long and hard riding and lean days. It was exactly how he was satisfied to look. His high-heeled boots of softly tanned leather were bespattered with the black mud of the marshlands to the west, and the more observant noted that the rain-caked dust in the dimples of his broad-brimmed "J.B." was the gray of the desert that rolled for desolate miles beyond the marshlands and the further hills. The tall "cowboy" had evidently come from quite a ways off and had come fast, or so gents with an eye for detail quickly concluded.

After swift, discreet glances the roisterers turned back to their drinks, their cards or their dance-floor girls. Too much curiosity where strangers were concerned was considered bad taste in the Gallo Rojo, and sometimes unhealthy. Only an old Mexican swamper, bowed in the shoulders by a life of toil, continued to glance furtively with awe-struck and worshipful eyes.

"El Halcon!" he murmured under his breath as he pushed mop and broom. Verily it is indeed The Hawk! El Halcon, the friend of the lowly! What brings him here, I wonder? *Caballeros de la Noche* — the Riders of the Night? Perhaps. But most certain it is an evil day for some — for some who are evil. El Halcon!"

Walt Slade did not hear the old man's muttering, but had he done so he would have been pleased, also

4

somewhat amused. For of El Halcon men also said, "If he ain't a owlhoot, he's got half the sheriffs of Texas figurin' him for one, even though they ain't ever been able to drop a loop on him."

Although this misconception often laid him open to grave personal danger, Walt Slade did not mind and did nothing to correct it, for he had found his dubious reputation often served him well in the course of his Ranger activities. Because of it he was often able to garner information from sources closed to a known peace officer, and he felt it was worth a little risk.

Slade found a place at the bar and ordered a drink. The barkeep eyed him respectfully as he downed the fiery liquor without the quiver of a muscle and poured another drink.

"Nice for a chaser," Slade drawled in his softly musical voice.

The second drink followed the first. "This one's on the house and then you get a free snake," said the barkeep, tipping the bottle.

Slade smiled with a flash of his even teeth startlingly white against his stubble of black beard.

"Thanks," he acknowledged. "I'll go easy on this one, and get the taste."

Lounging comfortably against the bar and toying with his third drink, Slade surveyed the colorful scene, from under his low-drawn hatbrim, with a much greater interest than his careless pose revealed. He quickly catalogued the place as a rendezvous for questionable characters, and questionable characters always interested Walt Slade.

The Gallo Rojo was crowded, although the hour was late, and more men kept pushing through the swinging doors. The bar was lined from end to end. Roulette wheels whirred, dice skipped and gamboled on the green cloth like spotty-eyed devils, chips clicked and gold pieces chinked at the poker tables. An orchestra on a little platform in a far corner played Mexican music and played it well. The clump of boots mingled with the sprightly clatter of high heels. The short skirts of the dance-floor girls swished a shimmering foam of color. The gay neckerchiefs of the cowboys and the silver conchas of Mexican vaqueros caught the light. Laughter, song, after a fashion, the whirl and patter of voices and the silky slither of shuffled cards cut through the thunder of the wind against the walls and the drum of hard-driven raindrops on the window panes. All in all it was a typical cowtown pay-night in a more than average lively saloon.

The appetizing fragrance of frying meat and steaming coffee drifted from the kitchen just off the bar and mingled with the pungent whiff of burning tobacco and the acrid fumes of spilled whiskey. While through the cracks in the roughly constructed walls seeped the salt tang of the sea.

Walt Slade felt the Gallo Rojo was a very satisfying place to be after the days and nights of hard riding that culminated in a battle with the storm.

Shouldering Slade at the bar was a big cowboy who was getting boisterously drunk. He roared discordant snatches of melody out of time with the orchestra, hammered the bar with his glass, bawled for drinks and

6

directed offensive remarks at the bartenders, who shrugged tolerantly but finally began casting inquisitive glances in the direction of Mexican Pete who, trim and elegant, lounged near the faro bank. Finally, at a nod from Pete, the bartender shook his head when the cowboy proffered an empty glass.

"Why not?" the puncher demanded truculently.

"The boss says no," the bartender replied and turned to serve a nearby customer.

The cowboy flushed darkly. He let out a string of oaths and hammered the bar.

Mexican Pete turned from the faro bank and sauntered over. He touched the irate cowhand on the elbow.

"*Señor*, you have had enough for the moment," he said in his soft, persuasive voice. "Come and sit at table with me and we will dine together. *Si?*"

The cowboy's reply to the courteous invitation was instant and violent.

"Get the devil away from me, blast you!" he bawled. His hand lashed out and caught Mexican Pete across the mouth and staggered him back a step.

Mexican Pete's pale eyes flamed in his dark face. His right hand moved with the flashing blur of a rattlesnake's stroke. Steel glittered and lunged upward in the deadly ripping slash of the expert knife wielder.

But quick as he was, Walt Slade was quicker. Fingers like rods of nickel steel clamped Pete's wrist, halting the blow in mid-stroke and slamming his hand down on the bar with numbing force. The knife flew from Pete's grasp and went spinning among the bottles. In the same lightning flicker of motion, Slade's other arm swept the cowboy backward and off his feet. He crashed into a table and hit the floor in a mad clatter-jangle of broken glass and splintered chairs, to lie stunned and motionless.

"If I hadn't stopped you, you'd have, been sorry about now," Slade remarked placatingly to Mexican Pete.

But Pete wasn't feeling sorry about anything just at that moment. His knuckles were skinned and bleeding from their contact with the bar, his lips were puffed from the force of the cowboy's backhanded slap.

"Meddler!" he hissed, and threw a wicked overhand punch.

The blow caught Slade squarely and sent him reeling and almost off balance. As if by magic, a reddened lump appeared on his cheek bone.

With an oath, Mexican Pete sprang forward, beside himself with fury. His second blow whizzed harmlessly over El Halcon's shoulder. Then Pete himself turned a flip-flop and hit the floor with a crash that shook the building. He bounded off it as if he were made of rubber and rushed again, swinging with both hands.

Slade met his rush in full stride. Toe to toe the two big men stood and slugged it out.

Fights were common occurrences in the Gallo Rojo, but not such a fight as this one turned out to be. Men were on their feet, crowding as near the battlers as was safe, whooping with excitement. Bets were freely laid and snapped up. Dance-floor girls screamed, the orchestra forgot to play, the bartenders hopped in wild abandon, yelling as loud as anybody else. Even the waxen-faced dealers at the gaming tables laid down their cards and craned their necks.

The two men fought silently, save for the panting of their breath and the thudding of their fists. Their faces were grimly set, but, in strange contrast, their eyes were smiling. Each seemed to be thoroughly enjoying himself.

Abruptly the end came. Slade's feet moved like those of a dancing master in a bewildering shift. With utter unexpectedness his right hand shot out, his left followed up. Once again Mexican Pete's long body shot through the air to crash on the floor.

This time he stayed there, his arms and legs moving jerkily, striving to rise but unable to co-ordinate his paralyzed muscles.

Walt Slade stepped back, breathing hard, blood on his face, his cheek puffed, the beginning of a "mouse" under one eye. He ran his bleak gaze over the crowd. Over to one side, half a dozen men who had been seated at a big table were on their feet, glowering darkly. Their hands flashed down.

Then they froze, in grotesque attitudes, gripping half-drawn weapons.

Walt Slade's slim hands had moved as moves the shadow of a passing falcon's wing. One fleeting instant of time and they were empty, the next they were clamped against his sinewy hips, and each held a long-barrelled gun, the muzzles of which yawned hungrily at the crowd.

Slade's voice rang put and now all the soft music was gone from it, it was the voice of El Halcon, bell-like, a steely rasp. "Start the ball rolling if you feel that way, gents, but quite a few of you won't be there at the payoff!"

CHAPTER TWO

Silence blanketed the room, silence broken only by the roar of the wind and the beat of the rain. Mexican Pete's supporters glared grimly, alert, watchful, waiting their chance. Disinterested bystanders began a mad scramble to get out of line. Slade turned slightly sideways so that nobody behind the bar could take him at a vantage. His thumbs snapped the big Colts to full cock, his fingers drew the triggers all the way back, so that only the weight of his thumbs held the hammers from falling on the cartridges.

"Well?" he said quietly.

An unexpected diversion occurred. Mexican Pete lurched to his feet and stood weaving unsteadily, blood running down his face, his back to Slade, directly in front of the yawning gun muzzles. There was nothing unsteady about his voice.

"*Puercos!*" he bawled at the tense group facing him. "Can not two *caballeros* have a friendly argument but you must seek to intrude? Since when have I asked others to fight my battles? *Vamos!*"

With sheepish grins the group dropped their hands and shuffled back to their chairs. Mexican Pete glared at them indignantly for a moment, then turned to face

11

Slade, who had holstered his guns and stood waiting. Mexican Pete approached him with an eager light in his eyes, like that of a child who hopes for a gift.

"*Capitan!*" he exclaimed, employing the Mexican title of respect. "It was that sudden shift of the feet and the unlooked for blow with your right hand that was my undoing! You will teach it me? *Si?*"

Walt Slade laughed aloud, his lips quirking merrily at the corners. "Sure," he chuckled. "Glad to. There's nothing to it."

Mexican Pete caressed his swelling jaw with tender fingers. "*I* have reason to believe there is *much* to it," he declared with conviction. Despite his puffed lips, his smile was singularly winning. He held out his hand.

Walt Slade took the proffered hand in a strong grip. The two stood for an instant, tall, lance-straight, smiling into each other's eyes. Then their hands fell away.

"*Capitan,*" Pete said, "first we will repair to the kitchen and wash away the blood and other signs of an honorable encounter, then I trust you will sit at my table as my guest, and dine?"

"Be pleased to," Slade accepted heartily. "I haven't really eaten for so long my stomach's beginning to think I've been hanged by the neck."

Mexican Pete chuckled and led the way to the kitchen. The big cowboy who had been the cause of all the trouble and was now much more sober than he had been, stared after them.

"Gents, I've a notion I sure got out of my class," he declared to all and sundry as he wobbled for the door.

After cleaning up a bit, Pete and Slade sat down at a table in a quiet corner. Pete ordered bountifully and as the waiter scurried to the kitchen, he smiled again at Slade.

"I hope you will pardon my outburst," he said. "I admit that I am somewhat fiery by nature, and when I'm irritated I am inclined to be violent, as you may have noticed."

Slade nursed his sore ribs and did not argue the point. Mexican Pete smiled and nodded. "*Muchacho,*" he called to the waiter, "bring wine, from my private cupboard."

Shortly, the dinner arrived. Walt Slade settled himself to it as does a man who has known what it is to find good food scarce. Mexican Pete smiled with pleasure and himself plied a busy knife and fork.

As he ate, Slade studied his table companion. Mexican Pete was a good deal of an enigma. He spoke unaccented English with an occasional Spanish word or phrase thrown in, somewhat in the nature of an afterthought, Slade felt. When he ordered the dinner he spoke Spanish to the waiter, and it was the Spanish of an educated man. Very pure Spanish, quite different from the current Mexican variety. Slade thought it came very close to being Castilian. In fact he began to doubt if Mexican Pete really was a Mexican. His English was not the stilted speech common to the Mission-educated Mexican. It was almost colloquial, saved from being so by a nice choice of words. And, Slade thought, there was an indefinable something

13

about him that hinted of the sea. He would not have been surprised if he had learned that Mexican Pete had been a sailor, very probably a ship's officer. And he thought, too, that the *conquistadores*, the iron men of Spain who conquered and settled a wilderness, must have been much like Pete.

Slade also quickly realized that Mexican Pete was one of those rare individuals who could talk a great deal and actually say little. Although he conversed pleasantly and fluently during the meal, he said nothing about himself, his antecedents, ambitions or activities. As they smoked cigarettes over a final cup of fragrant coffee, Slade knew he had learned nothing of importance about his host. He was more impressed than at the beginning that, Mexican Pete *was* an enigma.

They had not finished their cigarettes when a group of seven men filed through the swinging doors and clumped together at the bar. They were not prepossessing looking individuals at first glance, less so on closer inspection. Slade noted that some of them were breeds with Indian blood predominating. The majority, however, were not and were hard looking men with watchful eyes that swept the room as they entered. Mexican Pete regarded them a moment, his fine black brows drawn together.

"*Caballeros de la noche* — riders of the night," he remarked, observing the direction of Slade's glance. "They come from the marshlands and the hills to the west. Never do they ride alone. There are some who say they might well be members of the mythical Night Riders."

14

"What's the difference?" Slade asked. "The two expressions sound synonomous."

"The difference," Mexican Pete replied slowly, "is that many men in this section prefer to do their riding during the hours of darkness for reasons best known to themselves, while the Night Riders are supposed to be a band of outlaws preying on honest citizens. So it would be hardly fair to lump all riders of the dark hours in that category."

"Agreed," Slade nodded, "although doubtless there are some who would call that a fine drawn distinction."

"Many," Mexican Pete replied, "but I believe it is our American way to judge a man innocent until he is proven guilty."

"*Touché!*" Slade chuckled.

"*Mot juste* — the exactly right word." Mexican Pete smiled.

Slade smiled also, to himself. Evidently Mexican Pete not only understood French, he also spoke it, and correctly. Which was interesting, but did not lessen his enigmatical quality.

While he answered Slade's light banter adroitly, Mexican Pete's gaze had remained on the newcomers. He seemed to intercept some glance or gesture understandable to himself alone.

"Your pardon," he said, rising to his feet. "I would speak with those men."

He approached the group and was greeted with curt nods of recognition. For some moments he conversed earnestly with them.

Through the blue haze of his cigarette, Slade studied the group, not missing the covert glances cast in his direction from time to time. Riders of the night! Uneasy men to meet with on a dark night.

Although his scrutiny appeared casual, the men interested Walt Slade. For it was because of the Night Riders that Walt Slade was in the Palma coastal country.

"The chances are it's just another brush-poppin' owlhoot bunch, but they've sure been raising the devil over there of late, if the reports I've been getting are authentic," Captain Jim McNelty, Commander of the famous and far-flung Border Battalion of the Texas Rangers, had said to his Lieutenant as he dispatched him on his latest chore. "Appears there has been an epidemic of wide-looping, a couple of bank robberies, stages held up, some killings and so on. Sheriff doesn't seem able to cope with the situation and he and other folks have been sending calls for Rangers. They say the Night Riders, as some loco jigger named the scalawags, are stealing them blind and slinging lead promiscuous like. So I reckon you'd better amble over there and have a look-see. Maybe you can get a line on who's responsible. Then you can come back and I'll send over a couple of good men to clean things up."

"Why not send them first?" Slade asked, poker-faced.

"Oh, I can't have good men wasting their time just looking around," Captain Jim replied, equally blank of countenance. "Of course if you happen to run into the hellions and they fall over their feet chasing you and bust their necks, it'll save me the trouble sending somebody else. But don't let 'em catch you. They mightn't be nice to you."

"I'll try and keep in front," Slade promised and departed for his long and hard ride, leaving Captain Jim chuckling over his little joke and confident there would be no need to send some good men, with El Halcon on the job.

"Sure was a fine thing for the outfit and the folks of the state when that young feller agreed to sign up with us," he muttered, for Captain Jim had a habit of muttering to himself when alone. Lighting a cigar, he settled back comfortably in his chair and pondered the chain of events that was responsible for Walt Slade joining the famous corps of law enforcement officers.

After graduating from a college of engineering, Walt Slade had planned to take a post-graduate course, to round out his education before going to work at his chosen profession. But the loss of his father's ranch, due to recurrent droughts and blizzards, and the untimely death of the elder Slade, had made the plan impossible for the time being. So when Captain McNelty, his father's friend, and with whom young Walt had worked some during summer vacations, suggested that he come into the Rangers for a while and study in his spare time, Slade thought the offer a good one and had concurred. Long since he had gotten all and more from private study that he could have hoped to acquire from the postgrad work, and he had more than once put his knowledge of engineering to use in the course of his Ranger work.

But Ranger work had gotten a strong hold on him and he was loath to sever connections with the outfit, at least just yet. He was young and there was plenty of time to be an engineer. He'd stick with the Rangers for a while.

"Yep, a fine thing," Captain Jim repeated to his cigar, "a mighty fine thing!"

Mexican Pete came back to the table. Slade pinched out his cigarette butt and rose to his feet.

"Reckon a little sleep is in order," he observed. "Any notion where I can find a room for the night? I left my horse in that little stable across the street, and I'd prefer being close to him if possible."

"I have a few rooms upstairs, above the *cantina*," Pete replied. "They are not elegant, but they are clean and the beds are good."

"That will be fine," Slade said. "I'll slip over to the stable and get my saddle pouches and blanket roll and be right with you."

Walt Slade returned, and Mexican Pete led the way through the swinging doors and paused at another door which opened onto the street. Slade followed him up a flight of stairs and down a drab passage. Pete unlocked a door and lighted a lamp.

"Okay," Slade nodded, after a glance around the plainly furnished but neat little room.

"*Buenas noches, amigo*. I trust you will rest well."

When his host had departed, Slade crossed to the window and flung it open. A booming wind bearing on its wings a spittle of rain and the salty freshness of the sea filled the room. Slade stood at the open window and breathed deeply of the chill, damp air. He went to bed with the window open and the boisterous sea wind romping through the room.

In the saloon below, Mexican Pete sat down at the table and rolled a cigarette. He smoked thoughtfully, his brows drawing together. His head floorman strolled over to join him. He was a lean, slightly stoop-shouldered man whose colorless complexion told of a life little acquainted with the sun.

"Well?" he asked expectantly.

"Carnes, I don't know," Mexican Pete replied. "A hard man and an unusual one. I can usually draw a man out when I really try, but tonight I fear I met my match, or, rather, my master, just as I met my master in a saloon brawl. He talked freely enough, and said nothing, parrying with ease the indirect question that will as a rule catch even an alert man unawares. He would answer, yes, but the answer would leave me groping. The type of a person who, when he chooses, uses words which rather than reveal his thoughts conceal them. He has ridden far to reach this section. Why? One thing is certain, he is not accustomed to wear a beard. He scratched his cheeks now and then, as does one to whom the growing hair is an irritation."

"Some folks can grow quite a crop of whiskers in the course of a couple of weeks of riding when they haven't any time to waste on a razor," Carnes observed shrewdly.

"Exactly," conceded Mexican Pete. "I will wager that when next we see him, the beard will have been removed. He would not have betrayed his aversion to it had he grown it in the nature of a disguise. He is not the man to make such a slip. Be that as it may, he will bear watching."

Carnes nodded emphatically. "Reckon the boys at the big table are pretty well convinced they met their master at handling holster artillery," he remarked. "Blazes! I never saw such a draw, and with both hands. He doesn't pack that left-hand gun as a reserve, as most two-gun men do. It's either hand with him, or both."

"The question is, why is he here?" Mexican Pete reflected aloud. Carnes shook his head and didn't hazard a guess.

An old cowhand with hard, bitter eyes behind a great beak of a nose sauntered across the room and drew a chair to the table. At the moment there was an amused twinkle in the depths of the pale eyes. He looked the others up and down and grinned.

"Well, Pete, it looks like you took a shellacking," he remarked.

"I'd be the last to argue that, Toby," Mexican Pete answered.

"Well, don't feel too put out over it," Toby consoled him. "Better men than you or me have taken a shellacking in one way or another from that big jigger."

Mexican Pete leaned forward eagerly. "You know him?" he asked.

"Yep, I know him," Toby replied. "Betcha he rides a black horse, just about the finest looking horse you ever laid eyes on. But don't try to lay a hand on it unless you hanker to lose part of your arm; nobody else can touch that horse."

"He said he left his horse at the stable across the street," Pete observed. "But who and what is he, Toby?"

"Well, among other things, there are plenty of folks will tell you he's the singingest man in the whole Southwest," Toby said.

Mexican Pete's brows again drew together. "Something I seem to recall," he muttered. "What else?"

"There's plenty will tell you he's got the fastest and most accurate gunhand in the Southwest," Toby added.

"I've heard that said about others," Pete pointed out.

"Uh-huh, and when you hear it said about *him*, believe it," Toby said dryly.

"And what else, seeing as you're bent on horning us as much as possible before you really say something," growled Pete.

"Well, the Mexicans of the River villages all along the Rio Grande, and a lot of other poor folks, wouldn't think it a bit strange or wrong if a statue of him was put over a church altar along with the other images of the Saints, and I reckon they'd bend their knee to it more often than to the others."

Mexican Pete again leaned forward, his eyes snapping. "Toby," he exclaimed, "you're not trying to tell us he's —"

"Yep, he's El Halcon," Toby interrupted.

Pete leaned back in his chair and whistled through his teeth. Toby grinned maliciously.

"Reckon the Night Riders ain't going to be over pleased to know El Halcon is squatting in this section," he chuckled. "You know he's got a sort of reputation of horning in on things and skimming off the cream, and leaving a few gents with their toes pointing to the sky when he pulls out."

Mexican Pete and Carnes exchanged glances.

Toby grinned again, mockingly, and stood up. "Well, so long, gents, sleep tight," he said. "I'm going over to congratulate the boys at the big table."

"Congratulate them?"

"Uh-huh. They're still alive, ain't they?"

CHAPTER
THREE

Sometime during the night, while it was still dark, Walt Slade awoke, conscious of an unusual sound. The wind had fallen and the sea was quieter, so that noises other than the subdued murmur from the bar below were apparent. And the uproar of the saloon was muted because the hour was very late and most of the celebrators had stumbled off to bed.

For some minutes Slade lay trying to catalogue the sound that had roused him from sleep. Gradually he placed it as the creak of inadequately muffled oarlocks. For another moment he lay still, straining his ears as the thudding creak grew louder, then he dropped his feet to the floor and stole quietly to the window.

The sound was getting louder from out in the darkness of the bay. Apparently a boat was heading for somewhere close to the saloon.

Abruptly the sound deadened, as if some intervening object had deflected it. Slade realized that the boat had passed in behind the building. For another instant the creaking continued, then ceased. The oar beats had stopped.

As Slade peered and listened, there came a lull in the wind and he heard a low jabber as of high-pitched voices undertoned by gruff, peremptory tones that apparently growled a command. Instantly silence fell save for a faint scraping and scuffling that quickly ceased. Then the creak of oarlocks resumed, fading away into the darkness.

For some time Slade stood at the window listening and trying to pierce the darkness which was now abysmal. Nothing further interrupted the plaint of the wind and the sea. He frowned, shook his head and returned to his bed. What the devil, he wondered, was a boat doing in, back of the building during the dark hours just before dawn. The muffled oarlocks hinted at an intention to escape observation, if possible. It was reasonable to believe that some sort of cargo had been unloaded. Perhaps Pete was indulging in a little genteel smuggling. Well, that was the Customs people's headache. The Rangers usually didn't bother their minds about what was the concern of Federal enforcement officers so long as Texas law was not violated in the course of the operation. Slade went back to sleep.

The storm had blown itself out and the morning sunshine was pouring a golden flood through the open window when next Slade awoke. As he lay watching the play of light and shadow on the dimpled blue surface of the bay, a discreet tapping sounded on the door. He arose and opened it, and discovered an old Mexican swamper accompanied by a large tin tub and two pails of hot water.

"Nice service, old-timer!" the Ranger chuckled as he helped move the pails into the room. "Do this for everybody?"

"It is the pleasure to serve — El Halcon," the old fellow murmured in liquid Spanish.

Slade's gray eyes narrowed slightly. "You know me, then?"

"*Si, Capitan*, and so do others, despite the beard."

Slade grinned. "Reckon I might as well shave the darn thing off," he said. "Don't care for it much, anyhow. Haven't had time during the past couple of weeks, though."

"*El Capitan* has ridden far?"

"And hard. This looks to be a rather nice little pueblo."

"*Si, Capitan*, but death dwells here," the old fellow replied as he softly closed the door and departed.

Slade gazed soberly at the closed door. He felt the swamper had the right of it.

He had finished his bath and shave but was not yet fully dressed when a stutter of gunfire sounded not far off. The fusillade was followed by a wild shouting and more shots. There was a clump of running feet on the board sidewalk, a rippling thud of fast hoofs, still more shots and a babble of excited voices. Slade leaned out the window but could see nothing because of the bulging wall of the building. He finished dressing hurriedly and descended to the street.

Men were running along the waterfront and turning a corner a block or two from the saloon. Slade followed the direction in which they were headed and soon found himself on the main street of Palma. Some little distance down the street a crowd had gathered in front of a frame building. Careened against the opposite sidewalk was a bulky stagecoach. The driver's seat was unoccupied and several men were busy soothing the jittery four-horse team. On the sidewalk in front of the building lay a dead man with a blue hole between his glazing eyes. A second man, his shirt cut away and his right shoulder streaming blood, was receiving attention. Slade noted that the windows of the building bore the legend, Express Company.

"They say the hellions got a gold shipment that was to be loaded on the stage," an excited man was explaining to a new arrival as Slade approached. "They plugged the express messenger dead center and busted the driver's shoulder. The nerve of those devils! Pulling a holdup right here in town in broad daylight. They were gone a-skalley-hootin' for the hills before anybody realized what was going on. The agent and a couple of fellers threw some lead at them, but they kept going."

"I didn't know the stage was packing gold," remarked the new arrival.

"Guess neither did nobody else, except those infernal Night Riders," said the other. "There ain't nothing they don't know. 'Pears it was a dead secret, or so the express people thought, from what I can gather. The gold was slipped in from Mexico last night on that little sloop that anchored off-shore during the storm. The express company was sending it to the railroad this morning. Reckon it won't see no railroad for a spell."

"Which way did they go?"

The informant gestured toward the dark hills, flanked by marshland, which shouldered the western outskirts of the town.

"Hightailed into the brakes over there. The express agent scooted up the street yelling for the sheriff, but a powerful lot of good that will do! Those sidewinders know every trail and game track through the hills and over the marshes, and they've already got a head start. The sheriff might as well chase his own tail around in a circle."

"How many of them was there?"

"Seven or eight," somebody said, "with hats down over their eyes and neckerchiefs pulled up over their chins. Here comes the sheriff now. That's Lafe Secrets with him. Understand Lafe owns stock in the express company."

Slade had already noted the approach of the two individuals mentioned. The sheriff was a lanky old man with a stubborn jaw and intolerant eyes. He wore a big nickel badge on his unbuttoned vest. A heavy gun, butt to the front, hung on his left hip. The sheriff was evidently a cross-pull man.

Fast on the draw and slow on brains, Slade summed him up and turned his attention to the sheriff's companion.

Lafe Secrets was tall, well formed and distinguished looking. He had keen, dark eyes and well-marked features that at the moment wore a somewhat irritated expression. Under the circumstances it was not unnatural. The sheriff appeared to be in a very bad temper with everything and everybody. This also was not unnatural. He turned to fling a remark at a fluttery, expostulating little man who pattered at his heels and whom Slade presumed was the express agent. The sheriff did not take the trouble to lower his voice and Slade caught his words.

"You fellers are a bunch of bunglers," he declared angrily. "Every precaution was taken to protect that shipment and yet somehow you let somebody know it was coming in. Was anybody allowed to leave that ship last night after the shipment was landed? Were all those drunken sailors kept on board till this morning as I ordered them to be?"

"Nobody came ashore except the messenger who accompanied the shipment," the agent insisted.

"The messenger? Where the devil is he?"

"He's — he's dead, Sheriff Barkley," faltered the agent. "That's — that's him over — over there on the walk."

Sheriff Barkley shouldered his way through the crowd to where the dead messenger lay. He glared down at the bullet-mangled face and swore.

"And I suppose he made the rounds of the town last night, eh?" he rasped, whirling on the perspiring agent.

"I — I wouldn't be surprised if he was out for a while, though I don't know for sure. You see he'd had a hard trip across the bay, and —"

"He was not in my place, I'm sure of that," Secrets interrupted in a quiet, modulated voice.

"But I'll bet he did his drinking in Mexican Pete's rumhole," growled the sheriff. "It's an open-and-shut case. The messenger got drunk and talked, and somebody had big ears. They learned the stage would stop here at the station to pick up packages and were layin' for it. That messenger —"

Again Lafe Secrets interrupted. "Jake, stop it," he said. "The man's dead and can't defend himself. Find out for sure he was out drinking last night before you start accusing him. There could have been a leak someplace else."

"I'd like to know where!" snorted the sheriff.

"I would say it is your business to find out," Secrets replied dryly. "If and after you've learned the messenger wasn't running around drunk last night."

"I'll find out, and I figure I know where to find out," growled Barkley. "The stage company will have a heavy claim to settle. The shipment was in their hands when it happened," he continued, with a significant glance at Secrets.

"Don't let that angle bother you," Secrets answered. "The company is insured against loss. But no insurance will bring back that poor devil lying there on the ground," he added bitterly. "And I still think it was a mistake not to have guards on the coach."

"Guards would have served notice to the hellions that there was something worth-while on the coach," the sheriff defended his position. "Guards didn't save that shipment when the stage was overturned in Ricket's Gulch. They were shot down like settin' pigeons."

Secrets did not further argue the point. "We're wasting time," he said. "Get a posse together and let's try and trail them. I wonder if the messenger *was* drinking in the Gallo Rojo?"

"I'm going to find out," declared the sheriff, flushing darkly. "Come on."

"You're wasting time," Secrets repeated. "You won't learn anything from Mexican Pete. He's too much for you."

The sheriff's face reddened still more. "We'll see about that," he replied ominously and headed for the waterfront, Secrets' long legs easily keeping pace with him.

A man came running across the street, stopped the sheriff and spoke to him earnestly for several moments, gesturing toward the waterfront and toward the scene of the holdup. The sheriff listened intently, his frown deepening, apparently asked a few questions, nodded his head and strode on.

Walt Slade, after watching a hastily summond doctor dress the wounded driver's wound, and with a last glance at the dead man on the sidewalk, walked slowly back to the Gallo Rojo and breakfast. The concentration furrow was deep between his black brows and his eyes were somber. He was thinking of two things. First, the group of hard-featured men who had conversed briefly with Mexican Pete the night before. The garrulous individual in front of the express office who regaled his acquaintance with an account of the holdup had said that the robbers numbered seven or eight. There had been seven of the men Mexican Pete had called riders of the night. Just coincidence, no doubt, but Slade was not given to overlooking details, no matter how small or of apparently little significance.

The second matter which he considered was the mysterious boat with the muffled oarlocks which had so stealthily approached the back of the Gallo Rojo during the dark hours. That boat *could* have come from the sloop anchored out in the bay, the vessel that brought the stolen gold from Mexico, and for the purpose of holding rendezvous with somebody in or around the Gallo Rojo. Just the workings of coincidence again, perhaps, but something to think about. Well, if the dead messenger did get drunk in the Gallo Rojo the night before, Slade believed he could learn of it, even though the sheriff couldn't. As he left the scene of the holdup, he had noticed a shambling figure edging furtively forward to have a look at the dead man. It was the old Mexican swamper who brought his bath water earlier in the morning.

CHAPTER
FOUR

When Slade reached the Gallo Rojo and sat down at a table, he found Sheriff Barkley and Mexican Pete, who looked sleepy and annoyed, in a violent discussion. Lafe Secrets stood at one side, a silent but evidently interested spectator.

"And another thing," the sheriff was saying, "I just heard there was an outfit in here last night that sure answered to the description I got of those hellions who robbed the stage."

"Perhaps," Mexican Pete replied. "There were many men here last night, some I had never seen before. I do not ask my customers for credentials or intentions."

"No, I reckon not," the sheriff returned sarcastically. "Do you recollect anything about the seven jiggers I'm talking about?"

"Yes," Pete answered unexpectedly. "They had been here before. They requested accommodations for the night, but my rooms were already taken. They had a few drinks and departed, whence I know not."

"Yeah, and they 'departed' a little while ago, whence they don't nobody know, I'm willing to bet on that, and the bank's shipment with them. And you're sure that messenger wasn't in here drunk last night?"

"How the devil can I know for sure?" Mexican Pete said in exasperated tones. "The place was crowded, and about two-thirds were drunk. How am I to be expected to recall one particular individual?"

"You're never able to recall anything I happen to want to know," grumbled the sheriff. He glared around the room. His gaze fixed on Slade's face and he studied him intently for a moment then strode across to the table.

"Name's Slade, ain't it?" he barked.

El Halcon looked him up and down before replying. "That's what I've always been given to understand," he replied. "Reckon you have the advantage of me. I don't recall you."

The sheriff glowered. "I've heard of you," he declared accusingly. "Trouble busts loose wherever you show up — just like it did this morning. This town can get along without your kind."

"Reckon it managed to for quite a spell before I coiled my twine here," Slade admitted.

"I'm advising you to move on."

"Thank you, but I'm not taking it."

"Not taking what?" sputtered the sheriff.

"Your advice. Do you have anything else to hand out free?"

The old sheriff's face flushed fiery red and he began an angry reply. Lafe Secrets, who had strolled across the room, interrupted his tirade before it got well underway.

"There's no sense in all this, Barkley," he said. "We're just wasting valuable time."

33

"This feller's got a bad reputation," the sheriff said.

"Perhaps he has, but it's a free country," Secrets replied. "You can't throw people in jail or run them out of town just because you've heard stories about them, and you know it. Come on, now. Let's get started. I'm riding with you, if you don't mind. Come on, you can't do any good here."

The sheriff grumbled and muttered under his mustache but permitted Secrets to lead him away.

"I got my eye on you, feller," he threw over his shoulder at Slade as he passed through the swinging doors.

Slade chuckled and, glancing around, detected a similar expression of amusement on Mexican Pete's face.

The saloonkeeper sauntered over to Slade's table and dropped into a chair, his eyes still sparkling with humor.

"*Buenos dias*. I hardly knew you without the beard," he said with a keen glance at Slade's lean, bronzed cheeks. "So you're the famous El Halcon, eh?"

"Don't you think notorious is the better word?" Slade smiled.

"Depends on the individual viewpoint, I suppose," Pete returned. "I can sympathize with one who has the finger of suspicion directed at him. Quite a few people will tell you that I am the real leader of the Night Riders, if there is such an outfit. Others maintain that the *Señor* Clark Waters is their chief, principally because he is a comparative newcomer in the section and doesn't kowtow to the old-timers who have been accustomed to having the say in all things."

"Clark Waters?" Slade repeated.

"Yes," nodded Pete. "He owns the Cross C ranch, which he bought from old Tol Cavanaugh. It is to the north, beyond the hills, and slightly west, just north, of Lafe Secrets' Forked S, which is much larger and runs much farther west, from the coast to the edge of the desert, in fact. Waters bought from Cavanaugh a little less than a year ago. He also bought what stock Cavanaugh had left after liquidating most of his holdings preparatory to moving to Dallas where he planned to live with relatives. Waters soon began bringing in improved stock and his herd grew swiftly, too swiftly, some think. Also he dug wells and put in windmills to supplement his rather scanty water supply. And he ran wire, which did not set very well with the old-timers who own the Rafter K, the Barbed Five, the Walking R and other ranches of the section, this having always been considered open range."

"Waters is evidently doing what other progressive cowmen throughout the state are doing," Slade interpolated. "Doing it because they must. The day of the open range is drawing to a close and progressive ranchers are learning that free grazing cannot compete with fenced range. Barbed wire has come to Texas, and it has come to stay, and the sooner the old barons of the open range admit the fact and adopt modern methods the better it will be for them. What else were you going to say about waters?"

"Oh, nothing much, except the first reports of Night Rider depredations began coming in a few months after he settled here, and the leader of the pack is supposed to be a big tall man who wears a long black cloak. Big and tall rather describes Waters as, I suppose, it describes me in a way. I opened my place here about the same time Waters set up in business, so I share the suspicion usually directed at a newcomer."

Slade nodded thoughtfully. "And Waters doesn't get along with his neighbors?"

"Oh, he gets along with Lafe Secrets, I believe, but Secrets usually manages to get along with everybody. He's a congenial sort."

"Secrets an old-timer?"

Mexican Pete shook his head. "Settled here about three years ago, I understand. He bought his land from the state, but he grazes it open and gets along with the other spread owners. He's a good businessman, helped organize the independent express company with headquarters here and owns stock in the company. Bought the Dollar Saloon, which was on its last legs, and made a go of it. He's an energetic sort and an excellent mixer. Manages to keep on good terms with everybody, even Sheriff Barkley who's usually crusty as a steer with a short tail in fly time. Our good sheriff was in a highly irritable mood this morning, although one can hardly blame him, circumstances being what they are. Been just one thing after another for the past few months and he can't seem to make any headway against whoever it is that's causing the trouble. My opinion is that several outfits are working the section, just as they recently worked the country to the west and south. But the sheriff, and most everybody else attribute the outrages to the Night Riders, if there is any such outfit. Well, I have a few chores to take care of and then I'm going to try and get a little more sleep. See you tonight, I hope."

With a nod and a pleasant smile he left the table and a moment later passed through a door that apparently led to the rear of the building, unlocking it first with a ponderous key. Slade distinctly heard the click of a thrown bolt after he closed it behind him. Just what was behind that door, he wondered.

After finishing his belated breakfast, Slade crossed the street to the stable which sheltered Shadow, his tall black horse. He paused to glance at the sky. The morning blue and gold had been displaced by a flattened leaden arch that stretched from horizon to horizon, under which a rising wind was already beginning to wail. Apparently the storm of the night before had circled and was coming back or another was rolling in from the inexhaustible supply of bad weather to the southeast.

After seeing that Shadow was amply provided for, Slade strolled along the main street. The town was not large, but appeared prosperous. Which was not remarkable, seeing as it was the supply depot for a number of big ranches and besides was a port for coastwise ships and even those entering the Gulf from the Atlantic. Doubtless a large amount of goods was unloaded at Palma and transported overland to the railroad. Also there were gold and silver shipments from Mexico. Three of which, incidentally, had been subjected to robbery during the past two months.

As Slade returned to the Gallo Rojo he saw the old swamper enter the side door with a mop and a bucket. Ascending the stairs, he found, as he expected to, the old fellow cleaning the passage. He unlocked the door to his room and said to the swamper, "I would like to talk with you a moment, *amigo*."

The old man abandoned his mop and pail and entered the room. Slade closed the door, sat down on the bed and motioned the Mexican to a chair.

"Your name, *amigo*?" he asked.

"It is *Miguel, Capitan*," the swamper replied.

Slade nodded. "Miguel," he said, "I think you got a look at the express messenger's body this morning — I saw you in the crowd — was he drinking in the *cantina* last night?"

The swamper slowly shook his head. "No, *Capitan*, he did not drink. He was wet and cold and tired. He ate, and drank much coffee, but that was all. He did not approach the bar. After he finished his meal, he rented a room from the *Señor* Carnes, the head floorman. I conducted him to it, the room next to this one. I am sure he went to bed at once. He descended early this morning, ate and departed, doubtless for the stage station. He had not been drinking."

"You're sure of what you've told me, Miguel?"

"Yes, *Capitan*, I am sure. I knew the man well and could not have been mistaken."

Slade pondered the information, rolling a cigarette. Through the blue mist of smoke he regarded the swamper.

"Miguel," he said suddenly, "what do you know about the Night Riders?"

The old Mexican almost leaped from his chair. Sweat beads popped out on his face. He raised a shaking hand and plucked nervously at his lower lip. "*Caballeros de la Noche!* It is not good to know of them, *Capitan*."

Slade laid a reassuring hand on the old fellow's knee. His gray eyes were all kindness. "No, I suppose not," he admitted.

"They are *muy malo hombres*," the Mexican muttered. "A tall man swathed in a long black coat rides at their head. They slay and they rob, even as they did this day. Somewhere in the hills to the west they dwell, and he who opposes them, or seeks to learn of them — dies!"

Slade smoked thoughtfully. He was ready to agree with Miguel that the Night Riders were "very bad men".

The swamper rose and edged toward the door. "I may go now, *Capitan?* There is work that must be done."

Slade nodded. He realized the futility of trying to extract further information from the old man in his present state of mind, even granting that he really knew anything.

"Well, he had learned something of value. The leak had not been through the dead messenger. His thoughts dwelt on the mysterious boat which had

39

whispered out of the darkness, paused briefly in the rear of the Gallo Rojo and then departed toward the outer bay where the vessel bearing the gold lay at anchor. It was not beyond the realm of possibility that the boat had relayed the plans for transporting the gold to someone on shore. Of course, there were other ships anchored in the bay and the craft could have come from one of them. But just the same it was something to consider seriously. Slade wished he could get a look into the back rooms of the Gallo Rojo, but didn't know how to go about it.

Pinching out his cigarette he got up and leaned out the window, studying the wall of the structure. Constructed of rough-hewn timbers, the building was firmly but carelessly put together. There were wide chinks between the massive beams. The cracks had originally been calked with mud, but nearly all of the filling had long since fallen out. An inner sheathing of boards, very likely placed at a later date, made up the deficiency and rendered the structure weatherproof. The sprawling two-story bulk extended far out over the oily waters of the bay, the rear portion being supported by sturdy piles. Slade noted that nearly a third of the section over the water was windowless. Whether the end wall was blank he could not determine.

As he studied the wall of longitudinal timbers, an idea came to him. It looked like an active man could edge along the wall with fingers and toes in the cracks between the beams. As to whether the pattern maintained in the end wall he could not tell, but it was logical to believe it did.

In an effort to make sure he descended to the street and walked along the waterfront. However he could not gain a point where he could obtain a satisfactory view of the end wall He noted that jutting out from it was a squared beam about five feet long, probably intended as a support for a block-and-tackle or some other lifting apparatus. For Slade believed that the building had originally been a warehouse of some sort. Now it was probable that the rear third, windowless, was a kind of loft, perhaps devoted to storage of supplies essential to the saloon and restaurant.

But just the same he had an urge to get a look in the windows that quite likely pierced the end wall. He returned to his room to smoke and think.

CHAPTER
FIVE

As the posse rode westward over a stony track, Lafe Secrets suddenly turned to Sheriff Barkley.

"Jake," he said, "I think you were a bit harsh with that young fellow in the Gallo Rojo."

"Well, I don't," growled the sheriff. "That hellion is El Halcon, and if he isn't an out-and-out owlhoot, he misses being one by the skin of his teeth. Wherever he shows up trouble busts loose right off, as I said, and he's got killings to his credit, no doubt about that."

"Then why hasn't he been arrested and thrown in jail?" Secrets asked.

"Because he's so dadblamed smart nobody has ever been able to pin anything on him," snorted the sheriff.

"How about the killings?"

Sheriff Barkley looked a bit uncertain. "Well, it seems that every time he's cashed in some jigger, the hellion had a killing coming and he managed to get away with it."

"I see," Secrets said dryly.

The sheriff whirled on him irritably. "Now listen, Lafe," he barked. "Put things together square. Last night El Halcon drifts into town. He heads for that infernal Gallo Rojo. Him and Pete had a row, or so I was told. I figure that was a put-on show. Anyhow, they make it up and sit down at a table together and right off get plumb chummy. Then in comes a bunch of off-color scalawags. Pete goes over and talks with them and then goes back to the table with Slade. Okay! Then this morning a blasted hold-up is pulled off in broad daylight and right in town. And right while you and I were getting ready to go over to the station and make sure everything is okay. The timing was perfect and everything handled like clockwork. The sort of a chore only a plumb smart hellion could figure out and pull, and there's no doubt but El Halcon is smart, and Mexican Pete ain't no snide himself. Then we go into the Gallo Rojo and there's El Halcon settin' at a table and grinning like a cat that's just swiped a saucer of cream and sees the canary's cage door standing open. He was just settin' there laughing at us, dadblast him! And Pete, of course, knows from nothing. See how it adds up?"

"I never saw a cat grin," Secrets remarked irrelevantly.

"Then you never looked close enough," said the sheriff.

"You build up a pretty good case," admitted Secrets, "but everything is based on pure theory and, in my opinion, pretty far-fetched theory at that. And don't forget, plenty happened before your El Halcon showed up here."

"But that ain't saying he wasn't back of everything," declared the sheriff. "Reckon he figured he'd better superintend a real big job in person. Seventy thousand dollars in gold ain't chicken feed."

Secrets changed the subject. "That much gold weighs heavy," he remarked. "Should slow up those hellions a little. In fact, I think it is slowing them up. The iron marks are cut deep and the space between them is lessening. If we'd just gotten an earlier start!"

The sheriff glared at him, understanding perfectly the implied reproof. "If I'd gotten a line on where they were headed for from asking a few questions before we started out, you'd be payin' me compliments," he growled.

"I'm not criticizing you," Secrets denied. "I was just wishing we'd got started earlier. All right, here's where the trail forks. Which one are you going to take?"

"We'll follow the tracks," Barkley decided.

"Fine," Secrets agreed, his voice again dry, "only I notice there are fresh tracks cutting into each fork."

With an oath the sheriff jerked his horse to a stop. The posse jostled to a halt behind him. He glared at the offending hoof marks which scarred the soft surface of each fork, one of which veered sharply south, the other taking a northerly trend. It was an old trick but nevertheless a good one with which to baffle pursuit. The band had split up, one bunch packing the gold to safety, the other hoping to lure the following posse on their track and all ready to speed up, unencumbered by the weight of the metal, and lose the pursuit amid the maze of tracks and trails scoring the hills and marshlands.

"Well, which shall it be?" asked Secrets.

44

The sheriff's brow wrinkled querulously. "By going north they could figure to make the well-traveled trails where we'd lose the tracks," he said reflectively. "If they could keep in the clear till dark, and that'll come early on a day like this, they could slip into one of the towns, split up and have alibis all set. Plenty to swear they'd been there all day."

"Sounds logical," Secrets admitted. "It would be a pretty long ride southwest to Mexico, and they'd know we would have a chance to catch up with them. But if they did manage to keep ahead and get across the Rio Grande they'd know they'd be safe," he added thoughtfully.

The sheriff appeared to arrive at a decision. "We're heading south," he said abruptly. The posse got underway, riding swiftly south by west, with the deeply-scored tracks plain before them. Soon, however, the nature of the ground changed, becoming harder and very stony. Here the tracks were faint and for spaces would vanish altogether.

"But I figure we're on the right track," insisted the sheriff. "Speed up and maybe we'll sight the sidewinders from some hilltop."

Despite the rain, which was falling heavily, Slade continued to wander about the town. He located Lafe Secrets' Dollar Down saloon, which was well housed and had an efficient look. Here, he gathered, the sheriff and other officials, the more conservative elements of the town and the big ranchowners did their drinking. He went back to his room, irritated with the weather,

45

and drowsed until dark, when he descended to the Gallo Rojo and something to eat.

The posse rode back into town long after dark, weary, disgusted, wet to the skin, and empty-handed. Slade strolling along in the drizzle, watched them enter the Dollar Down in search of food and other refreshment. A few minutes later Slade also entered the saloon.

Lafe Secrets was standing at the far end of the bar conversing with a fairly tall, rugged looking young man in rangeland garb. He caught Slade's eye and nodded affably.

Slade saw Sheriff Barkley seated at a table, his back to the bar, busily putting away a hefty surrounding. Slade did not announce himself, fearing that to do so might spoil the sheriff's appetite. He found a place at the bar and soon became interested in the conversation at a nearby table. A couple of possemen eating there were regaling acquaintances with an account of their misadventure.

"I figure we might have caught up with the devils if Jake Barkley hadn't been so slow getting started," one was saying. "Those hellions were heavy loaded with all that gold. Seventy thousand dollars' worth weighs plenty and is hard to handle on horseback. And then he went and turned the wrong way at the forks. We followed the tracks south for six or seven miles till we came to another fork. There the sidewinders split again. We tried one and found it forked a couple more times, and at each one they split, until we were following just one horse and we didn't catch up with that one. Went back and tried the other fork that headed due west.

Same thing happened, only faster. By that time the rain was coming down like the devil beating tanbark and it was getting dark. We knew we were skunked and headed for home. I'm afraid Jake is getting a mite old and doddery. We should have selected a younger man last election."

"Reckon we would have if Lafe Secrets hadn't thrown his weight around in favor of Jake," the second posseman observed. "Lafe controls a lot of votes. Folks think sort of well of Lafe and pay attention to what he says."

"Got a notion he's feeling a bit different about Jake right now," the first speaker 'lowed. "He didn't say anything but I had a notion he figured the north fork was the one to take. Of course, him and Jake have been friends almost since Lafe first came here. And Jake used to be some punkins in a ruckus. It was him singlehanded who broke up that bad fight here in the Dollar Down last year and, the chances are, saved a killing or two. I reckon Secrets didn't forget that when election time rolled around."

"Yes, but a fast gunhand and plenty of nerve ain't always enough to make a first class peace officer," the other pointed out. "I understand the Rangers, for instance, know that a feller needs to be sort of long on brains, too. Bet yor, after what happened today, we get some of those fellers sent here to look things over. Understand they've already been asked for."

The other posseman nodded. "That's right, but the nearest Ranger Post is a long ways to the west, and the Rangers are sort of busy gents nowadays."

As Slade toyed with his glass, Lafe Secrets strolled up accompanied by the young man in rangeland clothes.

"Howdy," he greeted. "You should have been with us. You missed a beautiful ride in the rain. Wish you'd have been along. Would have given Jake Barkley something else to cuss."

"I've a notion he found plenty as it was," Slade smiled.

"You're right about that," Secrets chuckled. "Slade's the name, isn't it? I want you to know Clark Waters, my next-door neighbor. Clark figures you and he have something in common."

"That's right," said Waters as he shook hands. "You must belong to the Night Riders, seeing as you're new here. And of course I do, and so does Mexican Pete and anybody else who hasn't lived hereabout for a hundred years or so. Not being born in the section is a crime, or so it would seem."

"Don't pay any attention to him, he's sour," said Secrets. "He doesn't take kindly to being looked on as an outlaw."

Slade was inclined to think that Secrets might be right. Waters had spoken in a bantering manner but there was a look in his light blue eyes that hinted at displeasure with something.

"Ride up and see me if you get a chance," Waters continued. "My *casa* is ten miles to the north, the old one in a grove of live oaks. First you pass Lafe's Forked S; it's bigger and new. Mine's the next you come to.

48

Ride up and we'll plan some new deviltry to keep Lafe and the sheriff hopping."

"You're saying that like it was a joke, but dadblast you, I've a notion you're talking straight," growled a voice behind him.

Waters turned his head and glanced at Sheriff Barkley. "See!" he exclaimed pointedly to Slade. "He's all ready to throw us into the calaboose."

"No, I ain't," disclaimed the sheriff. "I've got reservations for a couple of honest horse thieves and I don't want them contaminated."

With a disgusted snort he stalked out. Lafe Secrets twinkled a glance after him.

"Don't be too hard on Jake," he admonished. "He's doing the best he can, and he always means well."

"Which is a polite way of calling a feller a son-of-a-gun," observed Waters. "Well, we're stuck with him and we'll have to make the best of it. Drop in and see me, Slade, if you happen to be riding up my way." With a nod he followed the sheriff outside.

"A rather nice sort, or seems to be," said Secrets. "And I doubt he's mixed up with the Night Riders or any other lawless aggregation."

"But you're not sure," Slade said.

Secrets shrugged his broad shoulders. "How can you be sure of anybody, considering the things that have been happening of late?" he replied frankly. "Well, have a drink on the house. I have a few chores to attend to."

He moved back to the end of the bar and conversed with his head bartender. Slade sipped his drink and studied the occupants of the room.

The Dollar Down was large, well-lighted and orderly. Local shopkeepers, and men Slade judged to be prosperous owners of the spreads to the north sat at the tables. There was a sprinkling of elderly cowhands, and several ship captains and their mates. A number of poker tables and other games were in progress. There was no music and no dancing. Sort of different from Pete's Gallo Rojo, on the surface, anyhow, Slade felt.

Shortly afterward, Slade left the saloon. He figured he had some time to kill and he didn't care to spend it drinking. He sauntered about a bit, the wind buffeting him, the rain stinging his face. And some distance behind, a blurred figure kept pace with him, following furtively, keeping always in the shadow of building walls. Finally he made his way to the waterfront, pausing from time to time to gaze out over the tumbled waters of the bay, where only the riding lights of ships and the phosphorescent tipped wave crests were visible in the black dark. Each time he paused, the furtive figure paused, always in the deeper shadow, and remained motionless and invisible till the Ranger resumed his slow stroll. It did not try to close the distance that separated them, but never did it lose sight of El Halcon.

CHAPTER
SIX

When he reached the Gallo Rojo, Slade did not enter the saloon. He hesitated for a moment, glanced keenly about and then slipped through the small side door and silently mounted to his room near the head of the stairs. He closed the door softly, purposely refraining from locking it because of the noise that would result from the squeal and click of the unoiled bolt.

Neglecting to light the lamp, he stood for some time at the open window, gazing into the wind-swept dark. Once he raised his head and listened intently, deciding, however, that he had only fancied hearing the sound of a floor board creak in the room next to his. Finally he removed his hat, his boots and his double cartridge belts with their holsters and heavy guns. He did not like to be without the big Colts, but if he should happen to slip and tumble into the water in the course of the adventure he contemplated, their weight would be an added hazard. He concealed boots and guns under the bed and returned to the window. With a last glance into the echoing dark he eased his body through the opening, feeling with his toes for the crevices between the timbers which formed the wall.

As he surmised, it was not particularly difficult to edge along the wall toward the rear of the building by way of the wide cracks between the beams, but just the same it was not a pleasant position to be in. Below, the black water sloshed and pounded against the piling. Above was the black bosom of the cloudy sky. The angry wind boomed and wailed between.

The gusts tore at his clothing. The wind-driven spray and rain beat against him. The old building creaked and groaned under the assault of the aroused elements. Inch by slow inch he edged along, rounding the awkward bulge of the wall and slowly approached the angle where side and end walls joined. A little more of this crablike progress and he made it. He craned his neck and peered along the end wall.

There were windows in the rear of the building, all right. Two of them, with heavy iron bars were outlined in a feeble beam of light that struggled through to glow on the black water below. The nearest was some six feet from where he clung to the wet timbers. So far so good. Looked like he'd be able to learn what, if anything, the locked back rooms hid.

And then, abruptly, it looked like he was not going to learn, not by the method he had outlined for himself, anyhow. As he reached around the corner in an attempt to find a crack into which to fit his fingers, his groping hand encountered tightly-fitted planking. The rear of the building was sheathed on the outside and there were no convenient crevices for fingers and toes.

Clinging with one hand, he stretched his arm out as far as possible, groping and pawing. No use! The planking was perfectly smooth, not even a toehold for a lizard. He glanced upward through the dark. No, that was no good. To try and climb up to the wet, steeply slanting roof would just end in him tumbling into the bay. Besides, even if he gained the roof he would be no nearer his objective. The windows were some distance below the peak.

As he hung against the wall, resting a moment before tackling the return trip, he was sure he heard voices, high, thin voices speaking words he could not catch. Confound it! There was somebody in that back room, and what the devil were they doing there at this time of night? His curiosity mounted to a white heat and he swore a baffled and disgusted oath. Only six feet of distance prevented him from getting a look in that lighted window, but it might just as well have been sixty miles. Muttering angrily, he began edging back toward his own window. He'd have to figure something else, just what he at the moment had not the slightest notion, but he firmly resolved to get a look in that window, one way or another.

After what seemed an endless shuffling and groping through the dark, he reached the window of his room and slowly levered himself up till his elbows rested on the sill. He tensed for the scramble through the opening.

Without warning, the room blazed light and sound. Slade was conscious of a terrific blow on the head. His muscles went limp, his grip on the sill loosened and he swayed backward. Through the windy dark he fell, toward the surging waves which reached up hungrily.

With a sullen plunge his body vanished beneath the black surface of the bay.

Down, down through the icy water sank the all but unconscious Ranger, his lungs bursting, his head ringing and spinning from the smashing blow dealt by the passing slug that just grazed his skull. He had just sense enough left to keep his mouth shut tightly and to refrain from breathing. Bands of scarlet fire and waves of inky darkness stormed before his eyes. He could hear the roar of the blood in his veins, the frantic pound of his laboring heart.

Down and down, his arms and legs moving feebly as he instinctively struggled to retard his progress into the watery depths. After what seemed an eternity of agonizing effort he gradually ceased to sink and began slowly rising to the surface.

For endless eons of pain and desperation he slowly, so slowly cleaved the pressing water, a clammy blanket of numb despair closing about him. His throat muscles swelled and tightened as his tortured lungs clamored for the surging gasp that would fill them with death dealing water. His arms were numb, his legs useless leaden weights that dragged him downward.

His suffering body could stand no more. His mouth opened. He choked, strangled, then suddenly gulped great draughts of dank, water-laden but life-giving air.

Paddling feebly with his hands, he managed to keep his head above the surface. The air was filled with rain and spray and he choked and coughed as he breathed, but filtering between the mist and water was the oxygen his bursting lungs demanded.

Slade's head still rang like a bell and he was sick and dizzy from the exhausting struggle and the blow of the bullet, but his mind was clearing, his strength returning. With a few faltering strokes he reached the piling which supported the building. He clung to the slimy posts until he could breathe freely and again co-ordinate his movements. By the time his teeth were chattering with cold and his limbs starting to numb from the icy bite of the water he felt equal to the task of swarming up the rough piles until he could get a grip on the wall timbers. The feat left him panting and with trembling muscles, but once his toes were in the crack between the first and second beams the rest of the task was comparatively easy. Just below the window ledge he paused to listen.

No sound came from above, but there was a faint glow of light seeping through the opening. Cautiously he raised his head until he could peer into the room. A quick glance showed the door standing open a crack. Through the narrow fissure struggled a beam from the single wall lamp in the passage. A moment later and he had assured himself that the room was unoccupied. He scrambled swiftly over the window ledge and scurried on all fours to the bed and dived under it.

His guns, boots and hat were where he had left them and apparently had not been disturbed. With a cocked Colt in his hand, he felt much better and wasted no time shutting and locking the door, which he belatedly realized he certainly should have done before embarking on his hazardous and fruitless journey of discovery outside the window.

Without delay he removed his drenched clothes and wrung most of the water from them out the window. He had a change of garments in his blanket roll and thankfully donned them. Warm and dry and comfortable once more, he opened the door and listened. A quick glance showed that the passage was empty and all the doors to the rooms closed.

A faint murmur of voices arose from the saloon below but otherwise the silence was broken only by the moan of the wind and the dismal slosh of the sea against the piles. He closed the door again and locked it. Then he sat down in a chair, rolled a cigarette from a dry supply of the makin's in his saddle pouch and reviewed the recent happenings. He blamed his own carelessness for the mishap. Things had been peaceful, so far as he was concerned, and he had been lulled into a state of false security.

The explanation of what had happened was simple enough. Somebody had trailed him, waited outside or in the next room and when they felt sure he was asleep had slipped in to do a finish job. Slade chuckled a little at the thought of how bewildered the would-be killer must have been when he didn't locate his intended victim in the bed or anyplace else in the room. And when he, Slade, suddenly loomed in the window, it was hard to tell who got the worse scare. Which was all to the good where he was concerned. Otherwise the hellion might not have jerked on the trigger, pulled his gun muzzle up a bit and shot high. Slade gingerly felt the swelling lump near the top of his head. The injury was trifling, the bullet barely cut the skin, but an inch lower and the sharks out in the bay would be having a feast.

All of which was a warning to keep his eyes open in the future and not take things for granted. He firmly resolved to do so, until he had another lapse of memory or again got too interested in some extraneous matter. But another such slip might well be his last one. Evidently somebody resented his presence in the section and intended to replace it with a void, if possible.

Who? Slade didn't care to speculate on that just yet. Too easy to make a profound mistake and possibly injure some perfectly innocent person, to say nothing of himself. But he was still extremely anxious to learn what went on in the Gallo Rojo back rooms. There should be a way to get a look through those end windows. Slade was determined to discover it.

Pinching out his cigarette, he left the room, carefully locking the door behind him, and descended the stairs. At the outer door he paused to glance keenly up and down the street, which at the moment was deserted. Loosening his guns in their sheaths, he entered the Gallo Rojo.

Mexican Pete was supervising the big faro bank, as per usual. He caught Slade's eye, nodded cordially, waved a greeting and turned his attention back to the game.

Leaning against the bar, glass in hand, Slade studied him in the back mirror and arrived at the conclusion that if Pete had anything to do with the shindig upstairs, he was certainly a fine actor. To all appearances he was totally unperturbed, at ease and free from any symptoms of surprise.

And Slade felt that when he walked in, to anybody mixed up in the plot, he must have looked like a ghost coming up out of the sea without getting wet. He rather hoped the sidewinder who took the shot at him was in the Gallo Rojo. If so, his present state of mind would be a rare sight could it be laid open for inspection. Slade suppressed a chuckle as his glance roved over the faces in the room.

A little later, Mexican Pete left the faro game and walked over to join Slade.

"I fear his ride in the rain did nothing to improve our good sheriff's temper," he remarked. "He came in a little while ago, his face like a thundercloud, and asked if anything was wrong in here, that he'd heard a shot and it sounded like it came from this locality. I told him that if there'd been any gun-slinging in here they must have used noiseless powder, for I certainly didn't hear any shooting and I'd been here all evening. He didn't seem to appreciate the humor of the remark. Then he asked if you had been around. I told him I hadn't seen you for some time. He didn't look convinced."

Pete paused to chuckle. "And then to make things worse, in ambles Clark Waters, whom the sheriff doesn't particularly care for. He asked Waters if he'd done any shooting lately. Waters said he hadn't but as he walked down the street he heard a shot somewhere in this direction. He asked the sheriff if he'd been

58

throwing lead at somebody. The sheriff didn't deign to reply. He just snorted and walked out. Waters said he'd intended going right upstairs to bed but when he heard a gun go off he thought he'd drop in and see if something had cut loose in here, because some of his boys were here playing poker. He's over at the far corner table with them, now. Evidently decided to see a few hands before going to bed."

"He's staying in town tonight?"

"That's right," Pete nodded. "He has the room next to yours, but don't worry, he won't disturb you. He's generally a very quiet sort."

"Quite likely, I'd say," Slade replied with a dryness that was lost on Pete.

Slade had been wondering if the shot had been heard in the saloon but decided it very likely had not. A healthy thunderclap would have trouble making itself heard above the Gallo Rojo's continuous uproar.

Pete went back to the faro bank. Slade centered his attention on the poker game in the far corner. The Cross C hands were lively-looking young cowboys who appeared to be enjoying themselves. A player with his back to the bar was no doubt Clark Waters. Slade could not see his face.

Mexican Pete's remarks had left Slade in a puzzled frame of mind. If Waters had been in his room at the time he couldn't have helped hearing the shot and would have known it was nearby. Slade had thought for a moment that he heard a floor board creak in the room next door just before he went out the window, but had not been sure. Now he was wondering. Of course there was no guarantee that Waters was in the room at the time, nor that anybody was, for that matter. Slade didn't know just what to think. But it was another aggravating loose thread joining the numerous ones that were already banging around. Beginning to feel the effects of his dousing in the bay and the strenuous activities that followed, he went to bed in a mood comparable to that which afflicted Sheriff Barkley.

CHAPTER
SEVEN

The sun was shining again the next day and apparently had decided to stick around for a while this time. Slade explored the town some more and encountered nothing of interest. He stood for a while on the waterfront and studied the rear portion of the Gallo Rojo. As his gaze rested on the stout beam projecting above the back wall, he formulated a plan that might give him a glimpse of what the back rooms held — a plan that might very well get him drowned if something went wrong. But nevertheless he resolved to risk it when what appeared to be a favorable opportunity presented itself.

That night when Slade entered the Gallo Rojo, he noticed a man drinking at the bar and glancing around the room as if in search of someone, a man who had a familiar cast of countenance. He studied the fellow under the shadow of his hatbrim and suddenly it came to him that he had seen the swarthy, hard-bitten face only a few nights before. He was one of the seven men who talked with Mexican Pete and whom Pete had called riders of the night.

As he ate his dinner, Slade watched the breed, for such he undoubtedly was. He had stopped searching the room and was giving all his attention to steady drinking, downing glass after glass of raw whiskey and, to all appearances, getting roaring drunk. As his actions steadily became more befuddled, Slade's interest increased. The fellow would either pass out soon or he would leave the saloon and doubtless head for bed. Where "bed" might be aroused Slade's curiosity, and it was not exactly idle curiosity. He might end up in the company of the other dubious characters who were his companions during his previous visit to the Gallo Rojo. Slade felt it might well be to his advantage to, if possible, learn something about the bunch. Sheriff Barkley was flatly of the opinion that they and the bunch which robbed the stage were one and the same. The sheriff might very well be wrong, but then again there was a chance that he wasn't. Slade decided not to pass up what might be an opportunity to find out. After he had finished eating, he pushed back his chair and with a last glance at the maudlin appearing breed, left the saloon, slipped upstairs and secured his saddle pouches, in which were some staple provisions, and crossed to the stable on the far side of the street.

"Reckon you're hankering for a bit of exercise and this may be your chance to get it," he told Shadow as he dropped the saddle onto his back and swiftly cinched it in place. He led the black to the door, opened it a crack and leaned against the jamb, his gaze fixed on the lighted entrance of the Gallo Rojo across the way.

He had not long to wait. Soon the drunken breed lurched through the swinging doors and weaved unsteadily toward the hitchrack a little farther down the street. He untied his horse from among several tethered to the rack and after several ineffectual attempts managed to mount the animal. Getting his feet firm in the stirrups appeared to be quite a chore, but he finally made it and rode slowly up the street, lurching tipsily in the hull. Slade waited until he turned the corner, then backed Shadow and rode in his wake.

The breed headed west, turned into the trail which led to the hills and rode on, slumping forward over his horse's neck, his chin sunk on his breast.

Slade followed, keeping well in the rear. The night was clear and starlit and the horseman ahead was a plainly-defined blotch on the white trail. Steadily he rode into the hills, never once looking back, lurching and sagging, apparently giving his horse his head and trusting to the cayuse's sagacity to keep him from going astray. Slade kept out of sound of the plodding horse's irons, losing sight of the quarry where the trail curved or ran in the deeper shadow but always picking him up again on the straight aways.

The hours passed, but still the drunken breed rode on. He was apparently fast asleep and it seemed a miracle that he did not pitch from the saddle. The east began to gray with the approach of dawn, but still he rode, never once looking back, seemingly entirely oblivious to his surroundings. He turned into the south fork of the trail.

The trail veered steadily southward, turning from the ragged fringe of swells and rises that bordered the marshlands and boring deeper and deeper into the higher and more rugged hills to the west.

Slade glanced uneasily at the brightening sky. It looked like the hellion was heading clean for Mexico. He wondered if the bunch had their hangout on the other side of the river. Well, if they could cross the Rio Grande, so could he. He had no official authority down there, but he'd take a chance on a little holster authority if it came to that.

The light strengthened and Slade dropped farther and farther behind. The trail was soft with the recent hard rains and the marks left by the irons of his quarry's horse were plain upon its surface. Unless the character of the soil should change, he could continue the pursuit by spoor without risking the chance of being observed.

The eastern sky changed from gray to pink, to primrose, to vivid scarlet banded with gold. The glowing rim of the sun showed over the edge of the world and the sky filled with light as a turquoise bowl with amber wine. Clear-cut, undeviating, the hoof marks led on.

Shadow topped a long rise and Slade caught a glimpse of the quarry, far ahead. The breed seemed to have shaken off some of his stupor with the coming of morning. He sat erect in his saddle and had quickened his horse's pace.

Slade drew rein and waited till he had vanished around a bend. Then he sent Shadow down the slope at a fast clip. He slowed him slightly on the upward winding beyond the bottom of the hollow and rode alert and watchful.

The bend in the trail was long and gradual. It was some time before it straightened out once more. A mile or so ahead was the crest of the rise. The game was nowhere in sight, but the hoofmarks of his passing still scarred the trail. Slade again let Shadow out till he reached the crest. He topped it and before him was a long level stretch devoid of life or movement.

Watchfully the Ranger glanced about. The trail shouldered a perpendicular wall on his left. To the right was an almost straight-up-and-down slope of earth and shale studded with boulders and jagged fragments of stone. It tumbled downward to the distant floor of a canyon where Slade's eyes caught a gleam of water. The opposite wall of the narrow canyon was less than a quarter of a mile distant, its rim thickly grown with brush.

"Shadow, that devil must have speeded up a lot to get out of sight so fast," he told his horse. "It's certain he didn't turn off anywhere unless he sprouted wings. Feller, there's something funny about this all of a sudden. I don't like it."

He shook his head and, keeping his mount close to the cliff and in the semi-gloom of its shadow, he rode on, more slowly now, with every sense alert.

The whole vista within the scope of his vision appeared peaceful and free from menace. The trail wound ahead, deserted, the distant canyon rim glowed in the strengthening sunlight, every twig and branch clearly outlined. Overhead the cliff wall towered in somber loneliness. Nothing moved, no sound broke the wasteland's silence. But suddenly, without any apparent reason, that uncanny instinct which develops in the brains of men who ride down the years with danger as a constant stirrup companion set up a warning clamor.

Walt Slade had long since learned to heed the seemingly senseless warning of this unexplainable, but very real monitor, that stood guard over him. Still nothing moved on the trail ahead. Still no sound other than the rhythmic click of his horse's hoofs broke the silence, but his flesh crawled with the feel of deadly peril close at hand. He crowded Shadow even closer to the stony bristle of the cliff and his eyes searched the distant canyon rim. Abruptly he went far sideways in the saddle and jerked Shadow against the cliff where an overhang cast an even deeper shade.

With a snapping crackle something split the air nearby and smacked sharply on the stony surface of the cliff. From the silent fringe of brush across the canyon, a puff of whitish smoke was drifting upward.

Slade slid his heavy Winchester from the saddle boot before the echoes of the distant shot ceased slamming back and forth between the rocky walls. He flung the rifle to his shoulder, sighted just below where the smoke was rising and squeezed the trigger. Almost instantly an answering puffball of smoke mushroomed up across the canyon, and another a little farther along the rim, and still another. Bullets yelled through the air and slammed the cliff face, one so close that it showered the Ranger with stinging rock splinters. He tried to ease Shadow still closer to the cliff and muttered a bitter oath.

Belatedly he realized that he had been led into a trap like a blind yearling. The breed hadn't been drunk at all but had simulated drunkenness so realistically that even El Halcon had been fooled. The hellion had eased him along all night to where his bunch was holed up waiting.

"And I fell for it" he wrathfully told Shadow. "I think my head needs examining — if there's anything inside of it to examine! If I hadn't seen the sun glint on that devil's rifle barrel as he shifted it to line sights with me, there'd very likely be a hole through it right now!"

Shadow snorted nervous agreement Slade fired again and thought he saw a sudden commotion in the brush of the canyon rim but couldn't be sure. More slugs came his way, some of them altogether too close for comfort.

Right at the moment the advantage was on his side, for it was doubtful if the drygulchers across the canyon would more than vaguely see him in the cliff shadow, but it would be different when the sun climbed higher in the sky. He was on a very hot spot and soon it would be hotter.

It got hotter even sooner than he expected, and from a totally unexpected quarter.

A bullet suddenly whistled past him, creased Shadow's glossy haunch and set him dancing and squealing with pain and fury. Slade whirled and glanced back the way he had come.

Nearly a dozen mounted men had just topped the rise less than a thousand yards behind. Smoke swirled up as they drove their horses forward at top speed. He was neatly surrounded!

More bullets from the canyon rim spattered the cliff face with lead. The men coming up behind were still too distant for anything like accurate shooting but that wouldn't last long and they continued to plump slugs toward the crouching Ranger in the hope of a lucky shot finding its mark.

Slade began to think very hard and very fast indeed. What was he to do? He couldn't remain where he was, that was sure for certain. Shadow would quite likely outrun the pursuit coming from the rear, but once he rode out onto the open trail he would provide a perfect target for the men holed up on the canyon rim. There was just one thing he could do, a mad gamble with death with all the odds against him, but to all appearances death was his portion no matter what he did. Okay! He'd take the desperate chance.

"Very likely we'll bust our necks wide open, but we're done if we stay here," he told Shadow as he whirled his nose toward the crumbling boulder-studded slope on the right. "Trail, feller, trail!"

With a snort and a squeal the great black went over the edge, plowing up clouds of dust, sending loose stones rolling, sliding and slipping on the yielding shale. At a wild run he went down the slope, keeping his footing by seeming miracles a dozen a second, staggering, reeling, losing his balance, catching it again, taking the steeper stretches of grade "settin' on his tail". Slade, swaying easily in the hull, guided and supported him, grazing him around jagged rock fragments, hurtling him over others to land on bunched feet and skitter crazily for yards.

From the trail above sounded yells and curses and a crackling of shots. Bullets stormed through the air, but the target was well nigh hidden by dust clouds and moving so erratically it was like shooting at a glancing sunbeam. Other bullets screamed from the far canyon but failed to find their mark.

Ahead was the gleam of water, but between it and the racing horse was a sheer wall dropping downward full fifty feet to the black, oily surface of a swift creek that rolled along the canyon floor.

"Take it, Shadow!" Slade shouted. "And here's hoping the water's deep and there aren't any rocks!"

Shadow didn't want to take it, but he took it, squealing with fright, his great muscles tense and rippling under his glossy hide. Down, down he rushed, his head tossing, his mane and tail rippling upward in the wind. He hit the water with a mighty splash and vanished in a welter of of foam.

CHAPTER
EIGHT

As Shadow's black head went under, Slade flung himself from the saddle but kept his grip on the bridle, shifting it quickly to the bit iron. A moment later both he and the snorting horse broke water. The current seized them and hurled them downstream. The men on the trail couldn't see them but bullets from the canyon rim spatted the water or whistled overhead. Another moment, however, and they were whirled around a bend and out of range.

But they had other troubles a-plenty. The creek ran like a mill race and the water was deep and cold. They were swept fully a mile downstream before, half drowned and well nigh exhausted, they swam and wallowed their way onto a little shingly beach and stood shivering in the warm sunshine.

"But we can't stay here," Slade panted as he strove to pump some air into his lungs. "Those devils on the rim may be able to make their way along it and be all set to line sights with us again. Blast it! I'm tired of getting doused in the drink. I hope this is the last time!"

Slade took time to pull off his boots and empty them of water, and to give Shadow a quick rubdown. Shadow whickered his appreciation and rolled a somewhat watery eye. With a chuckle, Slade mounted and sent him down the canyon as fast as his condition would permit. Very soon, however, the strength of both returned. Slade's clothes dried in the strengthening sunshine and he would have been inclined to laugh at the misadventure were it not for the rankling remembrance of how he had been duped by the wily breed. So far, he wasn't doing any better than Sheriff Barkley in coping with the situation prevailing in the section. Up to the present the outlaws had tried every trick.

As he rode, Slade managed to drain his saddle pouches and was thankful to find that his small store of staple provisions, which reposed alongside a little skillet and small flat bucket, had not been much damaged. Bacon, flour and coffee in waterproof packaging had suffered little hurt and some carefully wrapped eggs had marvelously escaped breakage. The same applied to his tightly-corked bottle of matches. At least he would be able to eat, when he reached someplace where it would be safe to pause.

The canyon bored through the hills for a number of miles, running south with a decidedly westward trend and it was early afternoon before they reached its mouth. Here Slade hesitated. If he turned east he would very likely hit the trail along which he had followed the breed, which evidently ran to the Rio Grande and Mexico, and that trail would take him back to Palma. But he had no guarantee that the outlaw bunch didn't turn and ride south in anticipation of his making just such a decision, and he had enough of those shrewd devils for one day. So he turned west, knowing that the range of hills petered out after a while and that he would be able to skirt them by way of level desert and rangeland and circle around their northern terminus and reach Palma by that indirect route. It would be a long ride but under the circumstances he decided it was the sensible thing to do.

Here at the southern tip of the hills he was close to fairly familiar ground, for it was by way of a trail that hugged the coast he had ridden to Palma. However, he still thought it best to stay west of the hills and ride north.

All afternoon he rode across rangeland and patches of desert. At sunset he paused to cook bacon, eggs and a dough cake and boil coffee. Shadow filled up on grass and Slade allowed him to rest for an hour before proceeding. It was long past dark but there was a moon in the sky when he was able to turn east in the shadow of the low northern slopes of the hills, following a traveled trail. Two more hours and he was passing clumps of cattle. And, as he rode where patches of thicket flanked the trail, he abruptly saw a band of horsemen filing down a track that ran from the south. Instantly he pulled up in the shadow of a clump of growth and watched the riders head for the trail. When they reached it they turned east, riding in a compact body. Slade let them get well ahead before starting Shadow moving again. He kept to the rear of the band, having no notion who they were, for there was a possibility they might be the very bunch which had so nearly cashed him in that morning. It was not beyond the realm of possibility that they had ridden south in the hope of intercepting him and were now making their belated way back home or to town or wherever the devil they might be heading.

Another hour and to the north the trail was flanked by strands of barbed wire. Evidently he had reached the beginning of Clark Waters fenced range. And ahead the clump of horsemen rode steadily with never a backward glance. Slade's curiosity mounted. It looked like they really were heading for Palma, where he might get a look at them. He took a chance and closed the distance a little. The trail was now curving south as it rounded the narrower northern straggle of the hills.

Another hour and he quickly halted Shadow. The bunch ahead had jolted to a stop.

However, they started moving again almost immediately, turning at a right angle from the trail, and Slade saw they were passing through a gate in the fence, which one had opened. His lips pursed in a low whistle. He rode forward a hundred yards or so and as the trail curved still more, he saw the dark bulk of a ranchhouse set in a grove of live oaks, into the shadow of which the band of riders was vanishing. He halted Shadow once more and sat watching the building. A few minutes passed and lights flashed through the windows. The mysterious horsemen were apparently the Cross C cowhands. What were they doing riding out of the hills, from the south, at this time of night? Slade earnestly wished he had the answer to the question.

For long minutes Slade sat motionless, watching the lighted ranchhouse until he was sure everybody was inside. Then he rode forward, slowly. He could see no signs of anybody outside the building. He quickened Shadow's pace and rode past, breathing a sigh of relief as nothing happened. He figured he'd had enough excitement for one day.

Five miles farther on he sighted another ranchhouse, a larger one and newer, which he knew must be Lafe Secrets' Forked S. And then, almost opposite the ranch-house, again he halted Shadow quickly and backed him into a thicket. Another band of horsemen, numbering ten or twelve, was riding up from the south. Slade muttered with exasperation. There was altogether too much traffic on the darned trail tonight. Tense and alert, he watched the slowly riding bunch draw near, their horses apparently weary. Slade thought one or two were limping. Mechanically he loosened his guns in their sheaths.

However, before they reached him, the riders also turned from the trail and rode toward the big ranchhouse. Slade relaxed. Evidently just the Forked S punchers riding in from town. A moment later he recognized Lafe Secrets riding in front.

Slade did not immediately ride on. Again he wanted everybody inside before he passed the building. If Secrets saw him he would probably recognize him in the bright moonlight, hail him and invite him in, and he had no desire to have to parry questions he would prefer not to answer. Finally, confident that nobody was still out prowling around, he spoke to Shadow and rode on at a fast clip.

74

Dawn wasn't far off when Slade reached Palma, but to all appearances the town was still booming. Although he was hungry, he did not pause until he reached the stable, looked after Shadow and then, too weary to do anything else, he slipped across to his room and tumbled into bed and was almost instantly asleep.

But even when on the verge of sheer exhaustion, El Halcon was a light sleeper. Less than an hour had passed and the pitch blackness that followed the false dawn was at hand when he was awakened by a familiar sound, the sound of muffled oarlocks whispering in from the bay.

Instantly he was out of bed and to the window, trying to pierce the darkness. The moon had set and the sky was slightly overcast, so that the veiled stars cast only a faint glimmer over the restless waters. He could see nothing, but the approaching sound steadily loudened. A moment later and it was muffled. The boat had passed behind the building.

The sound ceased. Slade strained his ears and to them came a low, confused murmur, high-pitched, almost like children's voices speaking under a blanket or a beetle droning inside a jug. Then there was a harsh, peremptory mutter and the murmuring stilled. Slade heard a slight and slithery scraping, as if something was being shoved against the rear wall of the building. It continued for a couple of minutes, there was a soft thud like the shutting of a door, then once more the muffled creaking of the oars as the boat faded back into the blackness that hovered shroud-like over the waters.

Slade listened until the sound had died and the silence was broken only by the lapping of the waves against the piles. Then, after another vain attempt to pierce the darkness while leaning far out the window, he grumbled a resigned oath and went back to bed. Something off-color was going on in or around the Gallo Rojo, there was no doubt in his mind as to that, but what the devil could it be. At present there appeared to be no answer. He drifted off to sleep again.

It was well past mid-afternoon when next he awakened. For some time he lay reviewing the day before's misadventures, and he was in a mood for self-censure. There was no argument but that he had been nicely duped and led into a trap by the cunning breed. And he felt that no credit was due him for escaping the closing jaws. Only a combination of luck and fortunate circumstances had saved him and the manner in which he circumvented the drygulchers didn't reflect favorably on either his astuteness or judgment. All the credit to be apportioned must go to Shadow. Were it not for the great black's courage, strength and agility, right now Walt Slade would very like be buzzard bait.

His mind eased by honest confession, he turned his thoughts toward the mysterious craft that had slipped up to the Gallo Rojo in the dark hours before the dawn. Out of the black sea it had come, and back into the black sea it had vanished. What was its mission? Would its appearance be followed by some outrage comparable to the gold robbery that took place hard on the heels of its former visit? Slade had an uneasy premonition that such might be the case. Well, if it showed again and he gathered knowledge of the event, he had a little plan that might give him an inkling as to its mission. He regretted that he had not already prepared for just such an eventuality. The night before was a lost oportunity.

Dismissing the nocturnal seafarer for the time being, he turned his thoughts to Clark Waters, the man Sheriff Barkley suspected of being mixed up with the Night Riders mythical or otherwise. What *had* Waters and his men been doing down in the southern hills that would bring them back to his ranchhouse long after midnight? How to obtain the answer to that, Slade at the moment had no idea, but he felt it was important to his personal well being and the success of his mission in the Palma country that he did obtain it. No wonder Sheriff Barkley was beside himself. Slade had a deep sympathy for the harassed old peace officer. To sympathize, one must undergo an experience similar to that afflicting the object of his sympathy. Slade was emphatically of the opinion that he was in a position to sympathize with Sheriff Barkley.

There was a certain element of wry humor in the situation and he chuckled more than once as he donned his clothes and descended to the Gallo Rojo for some badly needed breakfast. He sat down at a vacant table and ordered everything in sight.

CHAPTER
NINE

Slade enjoyed a leisurely meal, drinking large quantities of coffee and still pondering the circumstances and conditions confronting him. That somebody was heartily in favor of removing him from the picture was incontrovertible. That had already been definitely proven a couple of times. His presence in the section had alarmed somebody. Which, while it involved him in serious personal danger, Slade felt was to his advantage. Nervous, apprehensive folks are prone to make mistakes. So far it appeared the mistakes had all been on his side, but he hoped that unsatisfactory condition would not continue indefinitely.

Although the hour was still fairly early, the place was filling up. Cowhands sauntered in, spurs jingling. Several Mexican *vaqueros* were already at the faro bank, wrangling amicably over their bets, their silver *conchas* flashing in the light. At the bar were a number of gentlemen who looked like punchers but probably were not, or at least hadn't followed a cow's tail for quite some time.

These last interested Slade, who studied their faces whenever he got a chance. However, he did not recall having seen any of them before. They were certainly not of the bunch who had conversed with Mexican Pete, the bunch of which the tricky breed had been a member.

Mexican Pete put in an appearance. Looking urbane and debonair he engaged his floormen and bartenders in conversation. Spotting Slade he waved cordially but did not join him at once.

A couple of ship captains entered and took a table near Slade's. After them rolled nearly a dozen deepwater sailors who had brought their storm voices with them, for soon their bellowing caused the hanging lamps to quiver. Slade chuckled and ordered more coffee. It looked like the Gallo Rojo was in for a big night.

This did not displease El Halcon. No matter what Mexican Pete was or was not, there was little doubt that his place was a gathering point for all sorts of dubious characters, and drink, women and music set men talking, and under such conditions men who talk sometimes let slip things they'd otherwise keep buttoned tight behind their lips.

The dance-floor girls began to show up and a little later the orchestra filled in and took their places on the raised platform back of the dance floor. Mexican Pete walked over and engaged the leader in conversation. Slade noted that both glanced in his direction, the musician smiling and nodding his head. Pete also smiled and approached Slade's table.

"*Buenos dias!*" he greeted. Then, with great formality, "*Capitan*, I hear you play and sing exceedingly well. Will you not sing for me? I love good music."

Slade hesitated a moment, then nodded. "If the company doesn't object."

"Nobody will object, that I promise you," Mexican Pete predicted emphatically.

He led the way to the platform, Slade strolling after him, an amused light in his gray eyes. The orchestra rose and bowed to him as one man. The leader stepped forward.

"The *guitarra, Capitan?* Here is one most excellent."

Slade took the instrument and tuned it to his liking. He straightened up, slipped the silken cord across his broad shoulders. Mexican Pete strode to the edge of the platform and let out a stentorian bellow, "Silence, please!"

He got it. The babble of talk hushed, all eyes turned expectantly to the tall figure of El Halcon.

Slade smiled at them as he ran his slender fingers over the strings with easy power. A tentative chord or two, a whisper of low-toned melody, and then he threw back his black head and sang — sang one of the haunting, lonely-sweet, smile-and-tear laden songs with which the lowly peon of Mexico is wont to voice his sorrows and his joys, his regrets for what he has never known, his hopes for what he can never be.

Drinks and games were forgotten, the feet of the dancers were stilled, and as the great metallic baritone-bass pealed and thundered in the high-ceiled room, even the wind and the surging sea seemed to hush to listen.

80

With a crash of chords and a last high bell-note of melody the song ended, and was echoed by a storm of applause.

"Thank you," Mexican Pete said simply.

Over to one side, a grizzled cowboy furtively drew a calloused hand across his eyes. "I ain't sure for certain," he mumbled, "which'd hurt most — to have that big jigger shoot you or sing to you."

Slade was about to leave the platform when he noticed two men who stood close to the swinging doors staring at him in what appeared to be bewilderment. His eyes danced with laughter as they met with those of Clark Waters and Sheriff Jake Barkley. He waved a greeting and nodded to his table. The pair hesitated a moment, then walked over to join him.

"Sit down and have a drink," Slade invited.

Sheriff Barkley regarded him with a comical expression of personal injury as he drew up a chair.

"Slade," he grumbled querulously, "Why don't you quit 'sociating with off-color characters and practising with a pistol on your fellow-beings and settle down to the business of making music? You'd get rich."

"I second that last," Clark Waters added decisively.

Slade smiled, but did not otherwise answer. Conversation lagged till the drinks arrived, then Waters spoke.

"I was telling the sheriff about what happened to me night before last," he said. "I reckon he figures I'm just stringing him with a yarn to cover up my owlhoot activities, but it's the truth."

The sheriff glowered and snorted and regarded Waters with a severe eye.

"What did happen?" Slade asked.

"Some hellions cut my wire and run off nearly a hundred head of prime stock," Waters replied. "They had a long start before we found out what had happened, but we decided to take a chance and try and trail them. We picked up the trail without much trouble and followed it south through the hills — followed it clean down to the bay. And there we lost it. We combed the section for hours but never could pick it up again. Those devils, and the cows seemed to just sprout wings and fly away. Where they got to is past me."

"Slade in turn regarded him, speculatively. Waters, just where did you come from to settle here?" he asked.

"Upper Panhandle," Waters answered. "Got tired of fighting blizzards and losing stock by freezing every winter and decided to move south. I got a chance to buy my place cheap and took it."

"Then you're not overly familiar with the country down here?"

"Not overly," Waters admitted.

"And I suppose you brought your hands down with you and they don't know much about it, either?"

"That's right," Waters nodded. "But what's that got to do with my cows? Where did they get to?"

"I think the sheriff can answer that," Slade remarked dryly.

"In my opinion they're in Mexico, or on their way there," said Barkley.

"But, blast it, they couldn't swim them clear across the Gulf!" Waters protested.

"No, but they could be transported across the Gulf," Slade explained. "There are plenty of ships plying the coastal trade that are equipped to handle cattle, and some of them are not averse to making a crooked dollar. I'd say there was a ship waiting to load them when they reached the water."

Waters shook his head and swore. "I've a notion maybe I'd have done better to stay where I was and fight the blizzards," he growled gloomily. "This is one heck of a section! Well, I'm going to have something to eat. Was almost morning when we got back to the spread and I didn't feel much like breakfast when I got up with just a few hours sleep. Now I'm hungry.

"Bring us another round, and then a big order of hog-hip and cackle-berries, and I mean a big one," he told a waiter.

As the waiter departed for the drinks and the ham-and-eggs the rancher ordered, Waters stood up.

"I want to see Pete a minute," he said and headed for the far end of the bar.

Sheriff Barkley watched him go, then he turned to Slade, and again he wore an expression of personal injury.

"Blast it!" he snorted, "I can't help but feel that young hellion was telling the truth."

"I'm afraid he was," Slade agreed morosely.

And if Waters was telling the truth, what had looked like a promising lead had gone skalleyhooting. Waters' account of the widelooping provided a perfectly logical reason for him and his hands to be riding up from the south in the dark hours before the dawn.

Sheriff Barkley downed his drink after Waters returned to the table, wiped his mustache and stood up.

"Be seeing you gents," he said. "Try and keep out of trouble, Waters, and Slade try not to shoot anybody before morning. I'm going over to the Dollar Down to see Lafe Secrets. He wasn't around all day yesterday. Said him and his boys were busy up on his north pasture combing brakes all day and they went to bed early without coming to town. Showed up this afternoon and looked like he'd had a hard day, all right."

Slade's eyes narrowed a little as they rested on the sheriff's face. "You say Secrets was working his spread yesterday and didn't come to town?"

"That's right," nodded the sheriff.

"Then I guess I didn't see him in town," Slade observed.

"Guess you didn't," said the sheriff as he headed for the door.

Clark Waters chuckled over his ham and eggs. "I've a notion your singing sort of softened the old coot up," he remarked. "He was acting almost human. Reckon you should sing to him some more."

After he finished eating, Waters said good night. "I'm beginning to feel the need of a mite of shut-eye," he explained. "And if I stick around here, I'll get mixed up in something and not get it. Be seeing you again soon, I hope, and hope to hear you sing again."

84

Slade ordered more coffee and sat for some time smoking and thinking. Things didn't appear to be working out so good. Of course, there was an outside chance that Waters had made up the yarn from the whole cloth, for the purpose of alibiing why he and his bunch were sashaying around in the hills at such an ungodly hour, if somebody had happened to notice them. Yes, that was a possibility, but Slade had to admit that Waters' story rang true. Even Sheriff Barkley, who undoubtedly was or had been prejudiced against the Cross C owner, conceded as much.

But if Waters was to be eliminated as a suspect, who else had he? Mexican Pete, something of a man of mystery, whom Slade believed had once been a sailor and was certainly not the common garden variety of saloonkeeper? Well, still to be explained was the mysterious boat that slipped up to the rear of Gallo Rojo in the dark hours, making every effort at concealment. Until its mission was convincingly shown to be innocent, Pete would bear watching.

Nevertheless he wondered uneasily if by concentrating on Clark Waters and Mexican Pete he might be shooting wide of the mark. For another loose thread had suddenly inserted itself into the chaotic pattern and was banging around merrily — one that embodied a supposition apparently so preposterous that, for the time being at least, he refused to give it serious consideration.

He was still feeling a bit tired from the previous day's strenuous activities and decided that a little more sleep wouldn't go bad. He had made up his mind to what his next move would be and it would mean another long and hard day filled with unpredictable possibilities. He waved good night to Mexican Pete and went upstairs to bed.

CHAPTER
TEN

Early morning found Slade riding west into the hills, and he was in a very serious frame of mind. Captain McNelty had been very much in the wrong when he allowed that just another brush-popping outfit of Border owlhoots was operating in the Palma country. Slade was convinced that directing the activities of the bunch locally dubbed the Night Riders was a shrewd, ruthless and extremely capable individual with the ability to plan a project down to the most insignificant detail and then strike swifly and without error.

The gold robbery conclusively proved that. The timing had been perfect and the operation had been carried out smooth as clockwork and without a hitch. Very probably Sheriff Barkley had been carefully studied and his indecision and penchant for moving slowly taken into consideration. The sheriff had wasted valuable time with extraneous matters, as doubtless the outlaws knew he would. That had given them all the start they needed to make a successful getaway. During the chase the sheriff had followed the obvious course and turned south. The robbers, figuring he would do just that, had turned north, gambling successfully again on what the sheriff would do.

Yes, somebody very much out of the ordinary was running the outfit and quite likely somebody who stayed unobtrusively in the background most of the time, adroitly pulling the strings, setting the stage and mapping the campagin.

The attempted drygulching was another example of careful planning and patience that had lured even El Halcon into a nicely set trap, leading him on and on till his vigilance was somewhat abated and then striking with deadly swiftness. Also, the mysterious individual appeared to have access to information not passed out for general public consumption. Which indicated that he enjoyed a key position somewhere; most logically, Slade felt, in the town of Palma.

Well, one thing the two attempts against his life showed was that somebody was getting nervous and apprehensive of his presence in the section. Which, as he had previously concluded, should work to his advantage.

When he reached the point where the trail forked, Slade turned south. His objective was two-fold. First, he was pretty well convinced that the bunch had a hole-up somewhere in the hills or the marshlands and that the south trail led in its direction. Doubtless it would be well-hidden, but where mounted men pass back and forth there are almost always clues to their passing.

Secondly, conceding that Clark Waters' story of the widelooped cattle was authentic, it would appear that the outlaws enjoyed some sort of a nautical tie-up. A ship doesn't leave a trail, but it is not readily amenable to concealment and it can put in to shore only where conditions are favorable. If he could locate the landing place it might well afford him an opportunity for getting a look at the land division of the outfit. Or if he could positively identify the vessel, its crew might prove amenable to a little gentle persuasion and divulge information of value. Slade rode on expectantly.

Passing the spot where the drygulching had been attempted was a bit disquieting. Conditions were altogether too favorable for a repeat performance and he uneasily admitted that whoever headed the bunch might be perspicacious enough to reason that sooner or later he would pass this way again.

However, nothing untoward happened and the only disturbing manifestation was that afforded by the elements. The sky was graying and a strengthening wind was soughing up from the south. Looked like more bad weather was in the offing.

Slade rode on at a steady pace, surveying the terrain over which he passed with a carping gaze. Overhead the cloud wrack thickened. The wind increased in violence. All things were shrouded in a wan twilight.

The ride to the coast was longer than Slade anticipated and nightfall was not far off when, having so far noted nothing of significance, he sighted the cold gray shimmer of the sea.

Slade knew that he was approaching an arm of the great main bay that was locally known as Resaca Bay, through which coastwise ships, having passed Padre Island, and the shallow Laguna Madre which lay between the island and the coast, edged their way along to reach Palma.

Resaca Bay is rightly named, *resaca* signifying marsh, swamp. From where the surf thunders and crashes upon sunken reefs to where a range of granite hills rakes the northeastern skyline with crooked fingers of stone, desolate marshlands roll in wild confusion. To the west are more hills that march solemnly down the long curve of the bay. Farther to the east is rangeland swelling from the reeds and sedge of the marshes and shouldering on to the gold and scarlet of the rising sun. Hills shoot up suddenly from the dreary floor of the marsh, like startled wild fowl, their crests bristling and broken, their sheer sides scored by untold eons of wind and rain and beating sun.

Trails run across the marshland, trails that can be negotiated by those who are familiar with their tortuous windings, but for the unwary is sudden black water which foams up around the deceptive grass tufts that look firm and safe. And under the foaming black water is slimy mud that clings like the arms of an octopus, and bottomless sloughs of quicksand into which the lost wanderer sinks with silent swiftness, in his ears the mocking roar of the breakers and the thin cry of the startled curlew that rises to his strangled scream of agony and terror.

Men live in the shadow of the hills, men who take unto themselves something of the venomous gray of the granite and the sinister black of the treacherous water. They move mostly by night, shunning the brightness of the sun and even the gray twilight of the cloudy sky.

Resaca Bay is their vineyard and the wine they press runs red as blood and sharp as a whetted knife.

There are havens of refuge in Resaca Bay for the ships that ply across the Gulf and along the coast bearing precious cargoes, refuge from the storms that sweep in from the waste of blue waters, refuge for those who know the windings of the channels. But on clear days and in balmy weather, the hidden reefs and shoals have cracked the back of many a tall ship which sailed too close to the inhospitable shore. Resaca Bay is ominous even in the golden flare of the Texas sun or under the silver blaze of the Texas stars, but when the storms sweep in and the sky is a flat arch, leaden-gray or ebon-black, it is a place of terror indeed.

There is a trail which skirts the rocky shoreline, a trail from which can be heard the hoarse clamor of the bell buoys, from which can be seen the guiding lights atop the hills, but in the reek and fog of stormy weather, the clang of the rocking bells is deceptive as to distance and direction, and the feeble beams of the wood fires which provide the lights are caught up by the mists and reflected from their true position. Only sailors of long experience with the forbidding coast can hope to safely negotiate Resaca Bay in stormy weather, and even these sometimes come to grief.

Along this trail, under a slatey sky already streaked with the deepening shadows of late evening Walt Slade rode. The wind had fallen, but it was an ominous calm. At any minute it could be expected to blow again and from more to the east. There was every promise of a wild night.

Slade rode slowly, pausing from time to time to gaze across the darkling water and to study the forbidding coastline. Because of the inclement weather he rather doubted if any vessel would put in an appearance, but he was determined not to miss any bets. He might get a break.

The shadow-streaks in the sky broadened and deepened to ebon bands that quickly merged and overlapped. And still the ominous calm persisted. No leaf of the sparse growth stirred. No spurt of dust arose from the desertlike beach. It was as if all nature were holding its breath in fearful expectancy.

Far out on the tossing water, near the flattened curve of the southeastern horizon, a dark line, thin as the stroke of a draughtsman's pen, suddenly appeared. Slade surveyed it with narrowed eyes.

"Here it comes, horse," he told Shadow, "wind, and plenty of it. There's going to be hades around here when it hits. June along, we want to get off this sandbank before it's turned up edgewise."

He tightened his grip on the reins and rode east by north along the curve of the bay, toward where the loose sand was replaced by rocks.

Before he reached the beginnings of the stony ground the sand was flying in clouds. The mutter of the breakers had deepened to a sinister roar. High in the darkening sky the wind shrieked and wailed, dipping to earth in mighty blasts. The air was filled with flying yellow-purple shadows which thinned as the wind whirled skyward, deepened when the mighty gusts hurtled to earth again. All about were thickening

92

gloom, tumult and thundering sound. Tortured bluish mists swirled up from the surface of the marsh to mingle with the low flying wrack. There promised a fit night for ghosts and warlocks, for witches' carnival and the frenzied dance of goblins damned. And this grim land was a stage in harmony with the wild drama of the elements. To the north loomed the grim-hills, where bleached, unburied bones strewed the thickets and the rocky slopes. To the south and southeast the seething waters whereon pirates once held sway and men died in blood and pain. Far to the west stretched the pitiless desert, familiar with death in frightful forms. Due east, beyond the marshlands, rolled the rangeland that had been, and still was, a setting for conflict and tragedy. This was a land of legend and outlandish traditions, where fiction shook hands with fact and acknowledged defeat.

As Slade rode on, buffeted by the wind, drenched by the wind-driven spray, he became conscious of a sound piercing the reek of fog and flying water, the incessant clang of a buoy, as insistent and lonely as the bell that tolls for a passing soul, and were that metallic voice unheeded by any out there on the stormy water, souls would pass, for the buoy marked the waiting fangs of a deadly reef.

Atop a hill somewhere out in the wastes of the marshland a light flickered and glowed, now hidden by the swirling wraiths, not shining clear and white, a guiding light for any ship that might dare the storm or be caught in it unawares. Slade gazed at it a moment, then glanced out over the raving waters of the bay. His eyes puckered as he glimpsed a shadow object tossed high on a wave crest. Instantly, however, the dark closed down again and it was lost to view.

"Shadow, that looked like a boat," he remarked, but who in blazes but a plumb loco hombre would run a boat out into that mess! Horse, we've got to find a place to hole up a bit, where I can get a fire going and cook something to eat. I'm getting mighty, mighty lank."

Shadow snorted agreement and picked his way carefully in the gloom, testing the trail with nervous hoofs, blowing apprehensively now and then. Slade sympathized with him. It was no place for a fall.

The dark, towering bulk of a chimney rock loomed directly ahead. About its base was a straggle of thicket. As he drew nearer, Slade saw that the base was much broken and shattered. Talus had fallen from a jutting overhead which formed almost a cave. The great blocks of stone scattered about would provide an effective windbreak, the thickets wood for a fire; and a little coarse grass grew around the brush roots. Looked like a better shelter than he had hoped for, and now rain was beginning to fall.

"Take a helping and then come in out of the wet," he told Shadow as he loosened the cinches and removed the bit. Shadow took him at his word and began to graze. Slade soon had a fire going and food cooking and coffee boiling. Outside the wind howled and the rain pelted down, but the deep hollow was warm, dry and cozy. Shadow, hugging the shelter of the rocks, cropped meditatively at the sparse shoots of grass and appeared content. After a while he joined his master in the hollow.

Slade ate in leisurely fashion but with keen enjoyment. The heat of the fire beat back from the rock wall and he was perfectly comfortable. Suddenly, however, he raised his head in an attitude of listening.

Gradually he realized that it was not what he heard that distracted him from his food, but what he did *not* hear. Something was missing — something that had been one with the wild music of the wind and the sea. For a moment he was at a loss to account for the omission and unable to definitely place it. Then abruptly it came to him, he could no longer hear the hoarse and steady toll of the bell buoy. He listened for several minutes, but the sound did not resume. Doubtless the buoy had broken loose from its moorings and drifted away, he concluded, and went back to his meal.

He drank a final cup of coffee, steaming hot, rolled a cigarette and smoked thoughtfully. For some time he sat staring into the red glow of the fire, pondering whether to move on or spend the night where he was. Really not much sense in barging about in the dark, and it was easy to get lost on the marsh trails at night.

The wind had increased in violence while he ate, but the rain had ceased. He stepped from the shelter of the overhang and glanced at the sky. The clouds appeared to be thinning, for the moment at least. Over to the left he could make out the white flare of the beacon atop the unseen hill. It was brighter now that the wind had thinned the mist wreaths and the rain no longer fell. He glanced out at sea. And at that instant the clouds curled up like the edges of torn paper and a wild white moon funneled a shaft of light through the opening. Slade uttered a startled exclamation.

A moment later, heedless of the buffeting of the wind, he was hurrying toward the low cliff against which the sea raved and thundered. He climbed onto a jut of stone and stood staring at the grim tragedy in the making out there on the white-capped waste of black water.

A ship was in sight, a three-masted, square-rigged vessel of no great size, tossing and reeling under the beat of the wind and the inward sweep of the storm-torn tide. Even as Slade gazed, a rocket soared up from her deck — a signal of distress. In the reddish glare he could make out black dots clinging to the rigging and could see the froth of water breaking over her decks.

"Good God!" he breathed. "What ever made them put in there? A blind sheepherder could see it's a mess of shoals and reefs!"

As he gazed with horror-filled eyes, she struck. He saw her reel and stagger like a drunken man who has lost his footing. He could almost feel the crash which he could not hear. The mizzenmast went by the board, slowly at first, with the stately grace of a great lady bowing to a personage, then with a hurried ungainly rush as the lines parted and the stick snapped off close to the deck. The dots clinging to the rigging were hurtled far out to fall in wide, parabolic curves and vanish into the roaring black water. Slade tensed to the thin screams of terror he could not hear.

Again the ship reared high in the air, like a living thing in torment. Slade caught the gleam of copper sheathing as her bow pointed to the rolling bosom of a black cloud. And again she struck, shuddering from stem to stern, splinted woodwork flying through the air to mingle with the spray that spurted from the sunken reef. And again she flung high into the air.

Down she came a third time, and as she thundered upon the sea-drenched fangs of stone to wedge there under the hammering of the waves, the black cloud rolled over the moon, the beam of silvery light snapped off and the dark rushed down.

The surf crashed and boomed, the wind yelled with greater fury, the rain surged down in sheets. The sea and its dead, the splintered wreckage, the grinning, exultant teeth of stone were hidden from view. Only the white beacon atop the hill continued to gleam and glow in venomous, mocking triumph, like a murderer's eye through the blood-dripping veil of his hair.

CHAPTER
ELEVEN

Quietly, methodically, with unhurried movements, Walt Slade saddled up. He carefully inspected his equipment, made sure that every buckle was properly fixed, every strap free from possible fault. What he contemplated might well be his last ride if something went wrong. He mounted and turned Shadow's head away from the shore. There was nothing he could do to assist the unfortunates, if any remained alive on the battered hulk wedged in the iron jaws of the reef. He was unfamiliar with the coastline, had no means of reaching them. The strongest swimmer could not survive for more than a minute or two in that pounding surf with the tide running in like a millrace and the furious wind churning the water to maddened eddies and vortexes. He stared long and earnestly at the flaring beacon on the hilltop, trying to estimate its distance and direction. The mists were swirling about it once more, but its intermittent beam shone through for deceptive instants.

Slade's face was bleak as the granite crags and all the laughter was gone from his gray eyes as he urged Shadow inland to the brink of the deadly marsh.

For Walt Slade well knew that what he had witnessed out there on the black water had been no deplorable accident. Somebody had deliberately silenced the voice of the warning bell buoy. What he had glimpsed in the last flare of the twilight *had* been a boat, a boat manned by somebody who knew the reefs and the channels and was able to navigate them even in time of storm. Somebody, or several somebodies, had rowed out there and silenced the buoy. And the flare on the hilltop had been lighted to lure the ship to its doom. Doubtless the authentic beacon intended to guide a ship to a haven of refuge was several miles farther east.

Wreckers! With an utter disregard for human life, and, Slade was convinced in his own mind, members of the devilish band that had been plaguing the section.

And once again soon after the mysterious boat had eased across the bay to pause in back of the Gallo Rojo, the outlaws had struck!

But somebody must have been stationed on the hilltop to keep the flare burning, and if he could just lay hands on that sidewinder he'd pry needed information from him or know the reason why.

Slade knew that there were tracks across the marshlands and he trusted Shadow's sagacity and uncanny instinct to ferret one out even in the black dark, and there must be a track to the hill on which the beacon burned.

At the brink of the marshland the tall horse hesitated, fidgeting with his feet, craning his glossy neck. Finally he stepped out boldly, but with shiverings and querulous snortings. Slade could hear and feel the steady pound of his hoofs on firm ground, although all around him were weird sucking sounds and tremulous sighs. Now that he was out on the surface of the marsh he could glimpse furtive, flickering lights that rolled aimlessly about — balls of fire like the ghosts of murdered men pitifully seeking the rest that their tortured souls would never find. But high in the black air the beacon on the hilltop glowed with a steady light that was his guide.

Shadow was sweating now, despite the dank fingers of the wind. His progress grew slower and slower. He turned this way and that, his hoofs questing the windings of the trail that writhed like a wounded snake in torment but veered steadily in the direction of the beacon. He snorted in abject terror as one forefoot plunged in quaking, sucking mud. With a convulsive heave, he recovered, and crept on. Slade's iron grip was firm on the bridle, although he was sweating a bit himself, and his quiet voice reassured the nervous horse. His eyes, still cold as the wind that roared in from the sea, were fixed on the distant beacon. He was grimly determined to reach the hidden hill. Yes, there would be a man or men, there who were familiar with the treacherous coast and its deceptive channels.

Suddenly Shadow hesitated, stumbled, backed away from an unseen menace. An instant later Slade felt his hind quarters surging downward as the edge of the trail crumbled beneath his weight. With a sullen plunge the black's hind legs sank belly deep into swirling water. Screaming with fear, he struggled madly to regain his footing.

Slade left the saddle in a streaking flicker of movement. His feet hit the firm ground of the trail and he surged forward with all his great strength. For horror-laden moments he fought desperately to aid the horse in its struggle to escape the clutching fingers of the quicksand into which it was sinking. With a ghastly sucking sound like to the strangled breath in a dying man's throat, one hind foot came free from the mud which clung like a serpent's coils. Slade shouldered and heaved against the animal's straining flank. He felt Shadow's great muscles ripple and swell as he made a final desperate effort. An instant later and the black horse was on firm ground once more, shaking like an aspen leaf in the wind, his breath coming in choking sobs.

Slade leaned against the bronc's wet shoulder and wiped the cold sweat from his face. He, too, was shaking from strain, his heart pounding madly. For an instant he hesitated, glancing back the way they had come. Then his gaze lifted to the mocking beacon flaring in the black sky, his jaw set grimly and he swung into the saddle.

Shadow didn't want to go on, but under the gentle urging of Slade's voice and hand he stepped out again, testing the ground with a pawing forefoot, sniffing the wet air. He veered slightly to the left and stepped with greater confidence. Slade glanced at the beacon. They were diagonaling toward the elusive gleam and unless the hidden trail veered again they should eventually reach the hill and firmer ground.

And then abruptly the beacon sank, flared smokily and vanished. Slade uttered a bitter exclamation, pulled Shadow to a halt and sat straining his eyes into the darkness.

For long minutes he waited, but the white glow did not reappear. The fire had been extinguished. The night was black as pitch.

What should he do next? He debated returning to the coast but dismissed the notion. It would be tempting fate too far to try to retrace his steps across the treacherous bog and it was doubtful if anything would be accomplished by doing so. The rain still fell but abruptly the wind was swiftly abating, as it had a habit of doing in these latitudes. If anything was going on down there, it would most likely be over before he could hope to regain the neighborhood of the wreck. He was utterly lost, with no idea which way to turn, but he knew that he must be nearing the end of the marshland and the sensible thing would be to get out of the swamp as quickly as possible. The next misstep might not turn out so fortunately as did the last one.

"June along, horse," he told Shadow. "Anywhere, just so it's out of here."

Shadow stepped out cautiously, following the track that curved and wound until Slade lost all sense of direction. His only guide was the distant pound of the surf, but this was unreal and elusive and because of the tortuous curve of the coastline was not to be depended on. However, he was confident that the sound was diminishing, which indicated that they were drawing away from the lowlands.

Gradually, the boom of the breakers grew indistinct, died away entirely. Only the ominous marsh sounds and the soft hiss of the falling rain broke the silence, for now the wind was completely still. Overhead was the black bosom of the cloudy sky, beneath the black surface of the marsh, between which only death and the weird elementals of the night moved and had their being. Slade felt that he alone of living things was here in this primal desolation.

But Shadow appeared to gain confidence as he left behind the sound of the worrying waters. He lengthened his stride, ceased to snort and tremble. Finally his confidence was justified. Slade heard his irons ring on stony soil. He slipped back slightly in the saddle, a sure sign that the horse was climbing sloping ground. The gurgle and moan of the marsh waters thinned and lessened as they were swathed in layer on layer of the reaching dark. Slade heaved a deep sigh of relief as they ceased altogether.

Shadow was stepping out boldly now. He appeared to be traversing a trail that had recently known considerable travel. Slade strained his eyes to pierce the darkness. The rain had ceased and the clouds were thinning. A pale mist of moonlight seeped through and swiftly grew stronger. Objects, shadowy and distorted, began to take solid shape. Slade could make out trees and occasional clumps of brush. Again the hurrying moon struggled into full view and cast its silvery sheen over a scene of wild desolation.

Behind was the dreary expanse of the marsh, looking as alien to man as the star studded, cloud flecked sky above. From its vast surface swelled the rugged masses of the occasional hills, shadowy, gigantic. Slade could see that the swamp curved to the north and south around a gradually widening tongue of land over which he was riding in an easterly by slightly north direction. Far to the south was the tossing gleam of the storm-wracked bay. And directly ahead and a little to one side, looming ghostly in the wan light, was the solid bulk of a house.

It was a huge and ancient house ponderously built of gray stone and set amid a straggling grove of great trees whose branches were gnarled and wind twisted. Tall, thin chimneys soared above the gabled roof. The many shuttered windows looked like dead eyes with closed and wrinkled lids. Wide stone steps led to the shadowy veranda and Slade could make out the darker rectangle of a massive door which appeared slightly ajar.

The great building seemed singularly out of place here amid the universal desolation of the swamps, the anomaly accentuated by the smokeless chimneys and the shuttered windows. The grim structure seemed to be holding its breath in shocked recollection or sinister anticipation. Slade felt his flesh crawl as he gazed at it crouching there in tense silence amid the leprous trunks of the gaunt trees.

Suddenly he chuckled aloud. He was remembering a legend which said that here on the edge of the marshland Jean Lafitte, the Gulf pirate, had built a house in which he lived after he was driven away from Galveston. Much more likely it had been the spacious casa of one of the old Mexican *dons* who many years before grazed cattle on the rangeland to the east and north and who had a penchant for building their homes in outlandish places. But it could be the house of Lafitte.

"And they say his ghost still walks in it," he chuckled to Shadow as his eyes roved over the grounds surrounding the house and noted several outbuildings set at some distance, one of which appeared to be a stable and looked tight.

"I don't figure the ghost would hang out in the stable, horse," he continued, "so you might as well get undercover for the rest of the night. I'm just about tuckered and I'll take a chance on the house, if I can get in. Those chimneys say there ought to be a fireplace in there somewhere, and a floor board in front of a fire is better to pound your ear on than the damp ground. Suppose we look over the stable, it's beginning to rain again."

As he spoke, clouds began sweeping over the moon and once more wind-hurtled drops stung his face. Looked like the storm had accepted an encore and was coming back for a repeat performance. He moved Shadow on and a few moments later dismounted in front of the stable. The door swung open on hinges that screamed shrill protest and he led Shadow under the shelter of the roof. Fumbling a match from his corked bottle he struck it and glanced about. Stooping, he picked up some wisps of damp straw and twisted them into a makeshift torch. By its feeble smolder he made out a clean stall and feedbox.

It appeared that somebody had used the stable not long before. There was a heap of hay in one corner and a bin half filled with oats. Probably cowhands from one of the spreads to the east pressed the building into service as a line cabin at times.

Anyhow, Shadow was able to put on the nosebag and showed decided approval of this unexpected handout. After giving him a good rubdown, Slade improvised another torch, shouldered his saddle and pouches and stumbled through the rain to the house. The veranda boards creaked under his tread but appeared firm enough. The door swung open noiselessly, as if the hinges had recently been oiled. Slade lighted his torch and found himself in a wide hallway. An open door led to a lofty and spacious room furnished with but a heavy table and a couple of chairs. He noted with satisfaction a stone fireplace. A considerable quantity of wood was stacked beside the hearth. Undoubtedly riders had been hanging out here every now and then.

Soon he had a roaring fire going and his clothes drying before it He was about to stretch out comfortably on the floor with his saddle for a pillow and bask in the welcome warmth when, as the flames flared up brightly, something he had hitherto missed caught his eye. For a long moment he stood staring at the grisly thing.

From one of the massive ceiling beams hung a noosed rope.

The explanation of the noosed rope's presence was simple enough. A rope is often found hanging from the roof beams of a line cabin in desolate sections. By means of it meat or other edibles are suspended in such a manner as to be safe from prowling coyotes or other vermin, but Slade had never seen a honda fashioned as this one was. The running line did not pass through a simple loop or metal eye as does that of a cowboy's riata, but through an ominous bulk, turn on turn — the seven turns of a hangman's knot!

What in blazes was such a thing doing here, Slade wondered. He approached the sinister coil and examined it. The rope was comparatively new. A tug on it showed it firmly fixed to the ceiling beam. One thing was sure, Captain Lafitte didn't put it here. The twine was too new for that.

The loop was somewhat above the height of his own head. "Reckon they used it to hang tall jiggers," he chuckled to himself and went back to the fire. Doubtless the thing had been but the whim of some cowpoke with time on his hands who fashioned it for want of something better to do. Slade forgot all about it.

Stretched out on the floor, his head pillowed on the saddle, his guns placed close to hand, he smoked a comfortable cigarette and watched the shadows dance in the dusky corners of the big room. They crept stealthily forward as the flames died down, retreated as they flared anew. The rain beat on the closed shutters and the wind, which had risen again, wailed and moaned about the eaves but with lessening violence. Evidently the belated tail end of the storm was blowing itself out.

107

And as he watched the stealthy shadows and listened to the elemental voices of the storm, Slade thought of another of the legends of the house of Lafitte, the story purported to have been told by a wandering man who once slept in the house, perhaps in this very room, if this was the house of Lafitte. The wanderer awoke to see the gigantic form of the dead pirate standing in the doorway, booted and cloaked, the water of his ocean grave dripping from his broad hatbrim.

"Gold you shall have, if you follow me," said the ghost of Lafitte. "More gold than is good for any man. The treasure is mine to give. I paid for it with the substance of my soul. But you must spend it only for the good of others."

The horrified wanderer fled the house in terror, without waiting to learn more. But the legend said that the ghost of Lafitte still haunts the desolate house of the swamps, ever seeking someone who will retrieve his blood-stained treasure and spend it on good works, and so obtain for the pirate's tortured soul the peace so long denied it.

Chuckling at the absurdity of the thing, Slade drifted off to sleep. He must have slept for a long time, because the fire was burning low when he awoke with a start to see a huge man standing in the doorway, a man who wore mud-splashed boots and was swathed in a black coat, whose eyes glinted in the shadow of his dripping hatbrim!

CHAPTER
TWELVE

The form in the door was ghostly enough in appearance, but the cocked gun it held in its hand was solidly efficient, and the voice with which it spoke was businesslike and anything but sepulchral. "Just stay where you are, feller, and don't make a move toward those guns or it'll be just too bad for you."

Behind the figure crowded other men, some of whom held lanterns, the beams of which dazzled Slade's eyes. He saw, too, that the men, including the big leader, wore black masks over their faces, perhaps donned when they saw smoke rising from the chimney and weren't sure just who might be occupying what was evidently their hangout.

"Get on your feet, slow and easy," commanded the big man.

Slade obeyed. There was nothing else to do. And as he did so, the light from the lanterns fell full upon his face.

The big man uttered a sharp exclamation. He took a step forward, his head outthrust, peering through the holes in his mask.

"Well, hang me for a sheepherder!" he bellowed. "Talk about luck! Look at him, boys, look at him! The

109

hellion walked right into our hands! Will the boss be tickled pink when he hears about this! This horned toad had him plenty worried. If this don't take the hide off the barn door! The great El Halcon caught pounding his ear and waiting for us to gather him in! Talk about luck!"

The others crowded forward, peering, exclaiming.

"Face the wall you," the big leader ordered. "Get your hands up and keep them up."

As Slade turned, grimly silent but seething with anger directed at himself, steps crossed the room.

"Get those guns and lay 'em on the table, Slim," the leader ordered. "Shove that saddle over beside the long gun and the pouches. Lefty, look him over for any other irons or a knife. Careful, now, he's tricky."

Slade felt expert hands pat his pockets, feel under his arms and at the back of his neck for possible concealed weapons.

"All right, turn around now, and you can put your hands down," the leader said. "Don't try anything, though, or I'll let daylight through you."

Slade obeyed, still silent. The other's eyes glinted evilly. He reached up and gave the noosed rope a tentative tug.

"Old twine ain't been used for quite a while, but she's still plenty strong," he observed. "Reckon we'll have to shorten it a bit for this jigger, though. Nope, not now. We're saving him till the boss gets here. He'll want to see him do a dance on nothing. Slim, you and Lefty stay here. Lock this feller up and stay here with him till we get back with the boss. He's going to be

110

mighty pleased with this night's work. A nice hefty passel of dinero tied onto and El Halcon rounded up. Yep, this has been quite a night. All right, the rest of you jiggers, come along, we're riding. I've changed my mind about stopping here for a spell. The boss will be waiting to know what all happened and he'll be sore as the devil if we don't let him know about this streak of luck right away. He'll be free to move around more, now, and not have to stick close to headquarters because of this snooping hellion. Let's go!"

They clumped out and Slade was left with his two jailers. While one kept a wary eye on him, gun ready, the other crossed the room, unlocked an inner door with a ponderous key and flung it open. He wrinkled his nose and sniffed as a blast of drank air wafted through the opening.

"All right," he told the Ranger, gesturing toward the open door with his gun barrel, "get in there, and keep quiet."

Slade entered the dark room. The door was pulled shut after him and he heard the key turn in the lock. For several minutes he stood motionless, trying to pierce the darkness, which was relieved only by thin shafts of light that seeped through cracks between the ill fitting door and the jambs. His anger was at a white heat and he clenched his fists till the nails bit into his palms. He had been hunting for the outlaw hangout. Well, he had found it! But it wasn't likely to do him much good.

Recriminatory questions buzzed through his brain. How the devil could he have been so careless and

111

heedless? Why hadn't he been suspicious of the infernal place at once, instead of blithely concluding that it had been used as a line cabin by harmless cowhands? Why didn't it occur to him that characters of an entirely different sort might have frequented it? Why had he ignored the warning of the ominous noose dangling from the ceiling? He should have been on his guard. He had been convinced that the outlaws had a hole-up somewhere in the hills. Such men don't ride out of town in a body when they have some foray in mind, but by ones and twos to a gathering spot, a base of operations. And why didn't he see that this old shack was ideal for such a purpose? It was well off the beaten track, well hidden and with easy access to the coast for those who knew the tracks across the swamplands. That should have occurred to him at once. He reflected disgustedly that maybe he'd better turn to herding sheep. Sheepherders didn't need any brains, or so the saying went. Well, there wasn't any use beating himself over the head because of past folly. What he had to deal with was the unpleasant present and the unpredictable future, the last which might well be exceedingly short so far as he was concerned.

In the outer room he heard the table dragged closer to the fire, the scrape of chair legs on the boards and, a little later, the chink of a bottle neck on metal. Turning, he glided noiselessly to the locked door and glued his eye against one of the cracks between door and jamb. He had a narrow view of the table, at which the two men were now seated. They had removed their masks and revealed hard-lined, otherwised nondescript faces devoid of distinctive features, that looked vicious enough but rather stupid. One was blockily built, the other thin and gangling. Typical Border scum, he decided, quick on the trigger but slow at thinking. Which might work to his advantage if some opportunity presented. Not that any seemed likely to present.

The two men had a bottle between them and were drinking from tin-cups. Slade speculated them a moment, then turned back to the dark interior. Moving away from the door, he fished out a match and lighted it. The brief flare revealed a square chamber of no great size. A bunk on which were disordered moldy blankets was built against one wall. Otherwise the room was devoid of furnishings. The single window was shuttered and heavily barred with iron.

The match flickered out. Slade groped his way to the window and felt of the bars. They were solidly imbedded in the stone sill and though rusted were thick and strong. He examined the bunk and concluded it might be possible to wrench loose one of the side rails, which would provide something with which to batter the door. But with the two jailers alert in the other room, such a procedure would be rank folly. He kept the loosened rail in mind as a possible weapon when things should come to a showdown. He seated himself on the bunk and thought deeply.

Slade felt pretty well assured that when the rest of the band returned with the boss, that noose would claim another victim. He had little hope of leaving the grim house alive if he was unable to escape before daybreak. And so far as he could see, he had little chance of even leaving the locked room, much less evading the armed guards in the outer room. He was on a spot, but he'd been on spots before and didn't give up hope. One thing was becoming definitely encouraging, the sounds in the other room: the two men were becoming loud and garrulous. Evidently the liquor they consumed was getting in its licks. If they'd just drink themselves into insensibility he might get a break. He listened with pleasure to the thickening voice of one.

"There's another quart in my saddlebag — haul 'er out."

"Maybe we'd better take it sort of easy," his companion remonstrated half-heartedly. "You know the boss is a cold proposition."

"Ah, to the devil with it!" growled the first voice. "We can carry our likker. Nobody going to be here for three hours yet, maybe not that soon, and we ain't got nothing to do. That jigger can't get out of the calaboose. A horse couldn't pull those bars loose or shove that door down. Get the bottle!"

Slade smiled grimly as he heard boots clump unsteadily on the floorboards. As yet he did not see definitely how he would profit by the guards getting drunk but he was prepared to grasp any opportunity that might offer. He wondered if, when they grew a bit more befuddled, he might be able, by one pretext or another, to induce them to open the door. If they did he would at least have a chance to go out fighting instead of having the life strangled from his body like a sheep-killing dog. For a long time he sat quietly on the bunk, while the voices in the other room grew more and more maudlin and incoherent. Finally what was undoubtedly a snore rasped on the air. He rose to his feet and glided to the door.

Through the crack he could see one of the guards, the lanky one, sprawled across the table, his frowsy head pillowed on his arms. His companion regarded him blearily, muttered something unintelligible and drank from the bottle. A moment later he drank again, hiccuped loudly, set the bottle down uncertainly. He half turned to glance at the locked door, as though feeling the bleak stare of the Ranger's eyes and wondering if he hadn't better investigate the prisoner. Apparently he decided it wasn't worth the effort, for he turned back and regarded the bottle owlishly, reached out a hand to it, drew it back. A moment later his head also sank on the table and he snored in unison with his companion.

Slade struck a match and examined the door. It was massive, fashioned of thick planks that, while old and worm-eaten and in some places crumbling with decay, were still strong enough to resist any amount of battering with the crude tool he could obtain. The racket ensuing from such an attempt would arouse even the drunks in the outer room.

The lock was ponderous, its thick bolt passing under an equally ponderous hasp countersunk into the wood of the jam. The hinges were wide and thick and fastened with large-headed screws.

But as he examined the hinges Slade's eyes began to glow. He struck another match and peered intently at the bulky screws and the wood of the jamb into which they were sunk.

The door was much newer than the jambs, the wood of which was split and crumbling under the onslaught of the years. Slade could pick out pieces of it with his fingernail. He fitted the nail into one of the screw slots. It might work! he'd done it once before when confronted by a somewhat similar predicament, only that time there were no guards on duty and he didn't have to worry about noise or time. He had something that he believed would serve as a screwdriver.

From a cunningly concealed secret pocket in his broad leather belt he drew forth the famous silver star set on a silver circle, the badge of the Texas Rangers. He knew the badge was backed with steel and its curved edge would resist considerable strain. He set the edge in one of the slots.

The slot was barely wide enough to accommodate it but deep enough to insure a good purchase. Gripping the badge firmly with his slim, sinewy fingers, he slowly put on leverage. The screw resisted, did not budge. Slade jostled the improvised screwdriver back and forth and tried again. This time the screw turned a little, squeaking a tiny shrill protest as the lower surface of the head ground against the iron of the hinge. Then the two surfaces separated and the work became easier. After what seemed an eternity of patient effort he was able to draw the long screw from its bed.

Again and again he attacked the stubborn bolts. One after another they released their hold on the wood. But there were four screws to each hinge and some were

116

very reluctant to come out. Slade's hands were worn raw and bloody and the curved edge of the badge grew bent and twisted. He patiently straightened it by prying in the slots and went on with the tedious work.

On the lower hinge he had to work in a cramped position which made the task more difficult. And all the while his ears were straining for the sound of the approaching hoofbeats that would set all his efforts at naught. The shuttered window was graying slightly and he knew the dawn could not be far off.

Finally the last screw was out. With a deep breath of relief he replaced the battered badge in its pocket. He paused a moment to steady his nerves and relieve his aching muscles. He had the door under control but the real task was still before him. He must gain the outer room and get control of the situation there before the befuddled guards could swing into action. His guns lay on the table and it was imperative that he get hold of at least one of them before the aroused jailers could draw their own weapons. And such men, even in a state of drunkenness, usually slept as lightly as cats. Everything depended on the element of surprise and his own swift and sure action. One fumble and it would be curtains.

Drawing a deep breath, Slade gripped the upper cross piece of the door and put forth all his strength. The heavy barrier resisted his efforts and refused to budge. He stooped, got his shoulder under the cross piece and heaved mightily.

The door suddenly sagged, swung inward, twisting the bolt from under the hasp. The full of its ponderous weight crushed down upon the stooping Ranger. With a writhing twist of his powerful body he slid from under the tottering mass as it plunged downward to strike the floor with a thundering crash.

The two guards, shot from their drunken slumbers, surged to their feet, glaring wildly, hands streaking to their holsters.

In a single bound Slade was across the room. He seized the bewildered jailers by their throats, crashed their heads together and hurled them from him. Half stunned by the impact of their colliding skulls, they reeled off balance and before they could draw, Slade had grabbed one gun from the table. The room fairly exploded to a roar of sixshooters.

Second later Slade, blood dripping from the fingers of his left hand and oozing from a bullet cut across his right cheek, lowered his Colt and peered through the smoke fog at the two motionless figure sprawled on the floor.

Confident that there was nothing more to fear from the guards, he wasted not a second. Holstering both guns, he scooped up saddle, bridle, pouches and rifle from the floor and headed for the stable at a dead run. He breathed deep relief as a familiar whinny greeted him at the door. Shadow was still where he had left him. It was already broad daylight and the outlaw band might arrive at any instant. He cinched the saddle into place with frantic speed, made sure the rest of the rig was securely placed and swung into the hull. Stooping low, he sent Shadow through the broad stable door. And as Shadow's irons clanged on the trail, a sudden shouting sounded, and the metallic clang of a rifle.

CHAPTER
THIRTEEN

Slade heard the slug screech past and twisted in the saddle. Pounding up the trail from the marsh were a dozen or more horsemen, yelling and shooting as they rode. The two in front were tall, one swathed in a long black cloak. It was too far to distinguish features.

Leaning low in the saddle as the bullets hissed past, fanning his cheeks with their lethal breath, Slade gave Shadow his head. The great black snorted, stretched his long legs and fairly pounded his body over the ground.

But the pursuers were well mounted also and the bullets were coming dangerously close. Slade dropped the knotted reins on Shadow's neck, slid his Winchester from the boot and twisted around. His eyes glanced along the sights.

A spurtle of smoke wisped up from the rifle muzzle. The shorter of the two front riders, whom Slade was sure was the man who had done the talking in the house, plunged from his saddle to lie in a sprawling heap. The other jerked back sharply on his bridle and his faltering mount was engulfed by the other horses, causing Slade to mutter an exasperated oath. That was the hellion he'd wanted the next, slug to find.

It didn't find him, but it sent another man reeling in his saddle with a howl of pain and pawing at his blood spurting shoulder. Slade fired again and again as fast as he could pull trigger.

A horse went down, another hurtled over it to turn a complete somersault. The cursing pursuit pulled up in milling confusion.

Slade slammed the empty rifle into its sheath and gave his whole attention to riding. A few more shots were fired, but the outlaws were demoralized, thrown off balance, and the slugs didn't even come close. Shadow was in full stride now and barring accidents there was scant chance of his being overtaken even if the pursuit were continued, which Slade didn't think it would be.

He was right. A little later he glanced back and saw the band had dismounted around the fallen.

"Well, horse, we came out of that a lot better than I'd expected at one time," he told Shadow. "I've got a couple of skin cuts and that's all, and my neck is the same length it always was, and for a while I certainly didn't expect that condition to obtain much longer. Now, if I can just keep from pulling some other loco whizzer maybe we'll be all right."

Shadow rolled his eyes dubiously, as if far from convinced. Slade chuckled and eased off his knee pressure.

"Take it easy, now," he said. "I don't think we've got anything more to worry about from those devils. I managed to do for three of them, maybe four, and put a couple more out of commission for a spell, I figure.

I'm feeling a bit better, even though I have been muddling things like a sheepherder full of redeye. Sort of evened up the score, as it was, and I've a notion that sidewinder they call the boss is a bit jumpier even than he evidently was before. Bet you I can call his name in two guesses, maybe one, but I won't, not yet."

For nearly two hours Slade rode at a moderate pace, following the trail which wound north by west through the hills and apparently paralleling to an extent the irregular coastline. Finally he reached the rangeland and rode almost due north, veering only slightly to the east. The crooked track through the uplands had taken him well out of his way, but it had been the only route out of the hills, so far as he could see. As it was, the shadows were long when he at last sighted Palma and dusk had fallen before he had cared for Shadow and headed for the Gallo Rojo and something to eat.

He found the *cantina* buzzing, everybody excitedly discussing some event.

"Bad shipwreck down in Resaca Bay," the bartender who served him explained. "The Santa Rosa out of Tuxpan. They piled her up on the reefs ten miles west of Lavaca Light. Nobody can understand how any skipper could be so loco as to beat in close to the coast along there with the buoy bells warning him off and no guiding coastwise lights. A little coaster brought the word in a little while ago. The Captain said she was wedged tight on a reef and looked bad broke up. He put in as close as he dared and said he couldn't see any signs of life on her. Reckon he couldn't. If she hit during the storm every poor devil on her was most likely drowned."

The bartender glanced about, saw that nobody was in easy hearing distance and leaned closer.

"Something mighty funny about that wreck," he added in lower tones. "And I bet you that ship was packing valuable cargo. Sheriff Barkley was in a little bit ago and he sure looked worked up. He was trying to locate Lafe Secrets, who's out on his range somewhere and hasn't been in town since night before last. Secrets is a big stockholder in the express company, and a feller told me they're running around in circles over to the express office, nobody seems to know just why. But I bet you there was something on the Santa Rosa they don't want to see go to the bottom of the bay. Feller said they're geting a boat ready to run down there as soon as it gets light in the morning. They ain't doing that just to look the wreck over, and you can lay to it."

Slade nodded, his eyes thoughtful. He was inclined to agree with the drink juggler, and he considered what he had just heard decidedly of interest.

"Where's Pete?" he asked, glancing around. "Don't see him."

"Rode over to Carlson, north of here yesterday morning, to see some fellers about a deal," the barkeep answered. "Ain't got back yet, but I expect him in later."

Slade nodded again, downed his drink and sought a table. He ate heartily and then sat for some time, smoking and thinking, listening to scraps of conversation, studying the occupants of the room. Business was

122

picking up, the place growing crowded. But Mexican Pete did not put in an appearance.

After a while Slade pinched out his cigarette butt and left the saloon. He walked to the main street and headed for the sheriff's office. A light showed between the closed shutters. Slade mounted a couple of steps and entered, closing the door behind him.

Sheriff Barkley was seated at his desk. He looked up in surprise. "Now what?" he asked. "Been into some deviltry and come in to give yourself up?"

"I've been in the notion of giving myself up several times in recent days, but not in the manner you mean," Slade smiled as he took a chair the sheriff indicated. "You're alone here?"

"Yep," answered the sheriff, "but if you're figuring to pull a holdup, you won't find anything worth-while in the safe. Take a look if you want to, it ain't locked."

Sheriff Barkley spoke sternly, but there was a twinkle in the depths of his faded eyes. Slade chuckled but was instantly sober again.

"Barkley," he said, "what I'm going to show you and what I'm going to tell you I want you to keep under your hat. Not to be mentioned to anybody, and I mean *anybody!* Understand?"

"No, I don't understand," growled the sheriff. "What the devil are you talking about, anyhow?"

Slade slipped the battered Ranger badge from its pocket and laid it on the desk between them. Sheriff Barkley stared at it.

"Now where the devil did you steal that?" he demanded.

123

"Didn't steal it," Slade replied. "Captain Jim McNelty gave it to me, just as he gave you two black eyes and a busted nose, forty years ago, for putting a live bullsnake in his bunk."

"He's a liar!" roared the sheriff. "He never laid a hand on me. All he gave me was a knot on the back of my head with a boot he threw as I went out the door." He rubbed his grizzled thatch reminiscently. "Old Jim was sure plumb ac'rate with that boot! Well, I guess you're handing me a straight story. Jim would never have told that yarn to an owlhoot. Come to think on it, I have heard that his lieutenant is about six-and-a-half feet tall and broad in proportion. El Halcon, a Texas-Ranger. Now I've seen everything! And Jim sent you over here?"

"That's right," Slade replied. "He got your letter, along with a flock of others, and decided a little investigation was in order."

"Well, I'm sure glad to see you," declared the sheriff, "only I've a notion he'd ought to have sent about a dozen more, the way things have been going."

"I'm rather inclined to agree with you on that," Slade admitted, "but maybe we can make out."

"Got a line on anything, suspect anybody?" Sheriff Barkley asked.

"Yes," Slade replied. "I have two prime suspects, and not a thing on either one of them. Not perfectly sure which is the right one, so far, but I've a pretty good notion, and practically nothing to base the notion on."

"Sounds encouraging," the sheriff commented dryly. "Suppose you're not ready to mention any names?"

"Not yet," Slade answered. "Right now I want to ask a question or two. First, what of value was that wrecked ship, the Santa Rosa, carrying on her manifest?"

"About fifty thousand dollars in bar gold," the sheriff replied. "Shipped by the Amalgamated Mining Company, an American-owned outfit south of Tuxpan, Mexico. The express company is sending a boat down there in the morning to try and salvage it, before the marsh men or somebody ties onto it."

"They won't salvage anything except possibly the bodies of some murdered men," Slade said. "Barkley, that ship was deliberately wrecked — lured ashore by a false light, with the warning bell buoys silenced. The captain thought he was seeing Lavaca Light and heading into Lavaca Channel with the open water of the main Bay ahead."

"How the devil do you know that?" demanded the astonished sheriff.

"Because I saw it done," Slade answered grimly. He gave the sheriff a brief account of the tragic happenings of the night before, which had come so near to culminating in final tragedy for himself.

Sheriff Barkley abruptly looked very tired and old. "So they're going in for piracy, too!" he muttered.

"Looks sort of that way," Slade conceded. "Now another question. Who up here would know the Santa Rosa was packing that gold?"

"Nobody but the officials of the express company and myself were supposed to know," the sheriff said, adding, "but it looks like the knowledge was common property, as everything else around here seems to be of late."

"Could the knowledge have been relayed here from Tuxpan ahead of the gold-bearing ship, after she put out of Tuxpan?"

"Very unlikely, I'd say," answered Barkley. "The Santa Rosa was a fast little sailer."

Slade nodded. "That's interesting, and unless there was a leak down in Mexico some time ago, it sort of narrows a gap for me."

Sheriff Barkley regarded him with a puzzled expression, but Slade did not choose to elaborate his cryptic remark.

"Are you going with the salvage ship?" he asked abruptly.

"Calclate to," Barkley replied.

"I may want to go along, can't say for sure till morning," Slade said. "Think you can arrange it?"

"I'll figure some way to fix it," the sheriff promised. "Might say the jail is busted and I want to have you where I can keep an eye on you."

"Guess that would as good an explanation as any," Slade smiled. "Well, I'll be seeing you in the morning, if I decide to go. Can't say for sure right now. Things develop so fast hereabouts of late that there's no telling what will turn up before daylight."

"You can repeat that," grumbled Barkley. "I feel like a squirrel in a revolving cage, going around in circles and getting nowhere. Good night."

Slade returned to the Gallo Rojo and sat down at a table. He ordered coffee and a sandwich and looked

126

over the crowd, which had been augmented by numerous new arrivals. The wrecked ship still appeared to be a topic of conversation and he heard many wild guesses hazarded as to just how the tragedy had come to happen. However, he heard no mention of the treasure the vessel had been carrying. Undoubtedly the secret had been closely guarded, but not quite closely enough.

Nearly an hour later Mexican Pete came in. His clothes were travel-stained, showed evidence of a recent wetting, and he looked weary. Glancing about he spotted Slade and waved a greeting. He conversed with his chief floorman for a few minutes, spoke to his head bartender and then unlocked the door which led to the backrooms. The door closed after him and Slade was pretty sure he heard the click of a shot bolt. He waited around for some little while, but Pete did not reappear. Finally he left the saloon, crossed to the table and secured his sixty-foot riata, which he took upstairs to his room. There he carefully doubled and knotted the rope to give him a line about half its original length and laid it ready to hand. Removing his boots he stretched out on the bed, his hands under his head. He was very tired but anticipation of what might possibly happen helped him stay awake.

After the hours of storm the sky was brilliantly clear the night very still with not a breath of wind stirring. Sounds carried a great distance and Slade could distinctly hear a ship's bell far out on the bay tolling off the hours. From the saloon below came a confused murmur, with occasional shouts outside as somebody differed with somebody else over some matter.

The hours passed tediously and Slade lay half drowsing, but with his ears attuned to catch any alien noise. It was long past midnight when he heard the thing he had been listening for, the whisper of muffled oarlocks coming from the bay. He arose and went to the window. He could see far out over the starlit bay but there nothing moved save the phosphorescent-tipped waves that lapped against the piles, loud in the great stillness.

But the sound of the approaching oarlocks continued, drew near, deadened as the boat passed in behind the building. And again arose the confused murmur and a gruff admonishment to silence. Slade stood listening until he heard the diminishing sounds of the departing boat. He went back to the bed and reclined in drowsy comfort for more than an hour.

Arising once more, he assured himself that the door was locked, examined the shortened rope and made certain the loops fastened at the ends were in perfect working order. Then he coiled the twine over his shoulder and eased out of the window, searching with his toes for a crevice between the longitudinal beams. Another moment and he was edging along toward the rear of the building.

This time there was no welcome cloud bank to obscure the starshine and he knew that he would be plainly visible to anybody watching the building, and a prime target for some trigger-happy gent. Once he heard voices passing along the street and hung

128

motionless until they diminished into the distance before resuming his crab-like progress.

He reached the corner, peered around it. The dim glow again seeped through the windows that cut the rear wall. He glanced up, estimated the distance to the beam that projected from the roof peak. Clinging to the wall with one hand, he uncoiled the rope and with a sure, easy cast sent one end spinning upward and over the beam, swiftly paying out the slack.

The dangling far end of the rope swung in toward him. Reaching out he grasped it. With the utmost care he inserted his feet in the loops, gripped the double strands firmly and let go his hold. He swung out over the water, but not quite far enough. He knew he was taking a chance on another ducking in the bay, and more than that. If he fell, the splash would assuredly be heard inside the room from which the windows opened, and very likely a swimmer below would be looked upon with suspicion, with the possible spectator perhaps deciding it would be best to stop his progress with a slug.

However, the rope held in place over the beam and he began to "pump" as children do when standing on a swing board. Back and forth he swung, each outward sway bringing his a little closer to the window. Finally he was able to reach out with one hand and grasp the sill, straining every ounce of strength in his fingers to hold on. His backward motion was stopped and he slowly drew himself forward until he could peer between the iron bars which criss-crossed the opening.

He gazed into a big room which was dimly lighted by a single hanging lamp. There were bunks built along the walls and in the bunks fully a dozen men were sleeping — men with lank black hair, placid features and yellowish complexions.

For long moments Slade peered into the room. Then he let go the window ledge and swung far back toward the corner of the building. At the apex of the sway he was able to get a grip in one of the crevices to stay his progress. Carefully disengaging his feet from the loops, he thrust them into the cracks between the lower timbers and after hauling the rope down from across the beam, coiled it and looped it over his shoulder.

"So that's Mexican Pete's off-color sideline business," he muttered in tones that hinted at both amusement and exasperation. "The ornery rapscallion!"

CHAPTER
FOURTEEN

Slade chuckled as he edged his way back to his room and did not appear altogether displeased with what he had learned. In fact he wasn't. To his way of thinking, Mexican Pete was exonerated of any part in the recent devilish doings, and Slade was glad of it. He hated to think of Pete being mixed up in robbery and murder, and he was forced to admit to himself that Pete had never fitted into the picture properly. He might cheerfully shoot a man who crossed or angered him, but Slade just couldn't see the smiling *cantina* owner deliberately dooming innocent men to death in cold blood. Pete was busting the law, all right, but in a manner that was of little concern to the Rangers and which Slade was inclined to view with tolerance.

And now, he grimly exulted, he knew exactly who to suspect, although he had not one iota of proof against the man, and to make such a charge without ample evidence to back it up would cause him to be regarded as a lunatic, to put it mildly.

However, fairly content with his night's work, Slade went to bed and slept soundly till dawn. He descended to the Gallo Rojo, ate a hearty breakfast and headed for the sheriff's office.

Sheriff Barkley was already there. "All set to go," he announced. "So you decided to come along, eh?"

"Rather, it was decided for me," Slade answered. "We'll talk about that later."

"Okay," nodded the sheriff. "Come along to the wharf. A little sloop, the Isabella, a fast sailer of shallow draught will make the trip. A good man to handle her. Got a couple of fellers who can dive if we happen to need 'em, and I'm taking along a couple of deputies, just in case. Lafe Secrets and Horton, the president of the express company, are going along, too. They're interested, of course, seeing as the gold consignment was to their outfit for transport to the railroad."

The Isabella proved to be a trim little craft and she was all ready to cast off her lines when Slade and the sheriff arrived. Secrets and the others were already aboard.

Lafe Secrets looked somewhat surprised as Slade climbed onto the deck with the sheriff.

"Decided you were right about this young feller, Lafe," Barkley explained. "I figure he's okay and will be a good man to have along with us, so I swore him in as a special deputy."

"Guess you know what you're about," Secrets conceded, and apparently forgot the matter, for he moved over to talk with Horton, the express company president, a corpulent individual with a normally cheerful countenance which was now lined by worry.

Sheriff Barkley beckoned to a huge and hairy man with massive bare arms that were stained by tar, thick shoulders and a choleric blue eye.

132

"Slade, want you to know Skipper Jack Bowen, who runs this outfit," the sheriff said. "Jack, here's a feller even bigger than you."

Slade shook hands with the skipper, and liked him. It appeared Skipper Jack reciprocated, for he grinned ferociously and twinkled his eyes at El Halcon.

"Glad to have you along, son," he boomed. "You look like you might pack a cargo of brains, which is more'n I can say for this old coot and those lubbers he brought with him."

"All right!" he bellowed to his crew. "Let's get going or it'll be dark before we come alongside the Santa Rosa, or what's left of her."

The Isabella tacked out of the harbor, caught the full force of the easterly breeze and heeled over. A spin of the wheel and she was running before the wind, a white bone in her teeth and her wake a flame in the blazing sunlight.

Slade stood by the starboard rail and watched the desolate coast slip past. Presently Skipper Jack Bowen rolled over to join him. The sheriff lurched and swore as the deck reeled, but Slade stood firm and easy on his feet, swaying lithely to the motion of the ship.

Skipper Jack shot him an approving glance. "Not the first time you've been on water, eh?" he remarked.

"Not exactly," Slade conceded smilingly.

Sheriff Jack nodded. "And there's another over there who knows what it is to have a deck under his feet," he observed, jerking his thumb toward Lafe Secrets.

"I've a notion you're right," Slade agreed thoughtfully, and changed the subject. "She trims nicely," he commented apropos of the Isabella.

"She ain't bad, she ain't bad," Skipper Jack agreed. "I brought her across through the storm the other night and didn't ship a cupful."

Slade smiled and glanced sideways at the big captain. He was of the opinion that Skipper Jack's seamanship had played a large part in making a dry crossing of the hazardous Gulf and bay.

Two hours and the bleak hills and occasional stone out-croppings that resembled chimney rocks of Resaca Marsh hove into view. A little later Bowen pointed to a hill that heaved its height from the venomous gray of the swamp.

"That's Lavaca Light," he said. "Right over there, where you see the cove, is a snug little harbor with clear water running right up to it. That's where the Santa Rosa should have put in if she was scairt she couldn't weather the storm to Palma. The devil only knows how they came so nigh to the coast over to the west."

"No lights over there?" Slade asked.

"Heck, no!" replied the captain. "Beacons are the last thing you'd want over there. Beacons are to guide a ship to harbor. Some day there may be regular lighthouses to mark the shoals, but now you couldn't get anybody to tend one in that foresaken swamp. Warning buoys, though. They should have veered off when they heard the bells. A Mexican skipper, though, I understand, and maybe his first trip along this way. Hugging the coast, like coastwise men have a habit of

134

doing, I reckon, and one of the currents caught him. Bad all the way along here. The reefs and the shoals, with deep water between them, make for currents that set in to land and if a ship, 'specially a small one, gets caught in one of those big currents, it's mighty apt to throw her on the rocks."

Slade gazed at the lanes of swirling black water with the surf booming up on all sides in a frothing madness, with eddies and vortexes spouting and boiling. Even a landsman, and Walt Slade had had some experience on the water in his younger days, could understand what scant chance a small vessel would have if caught in the grip of that terrific suction.

"I'm going to take the wheel now," said Bowen. "That swab'll pile her up in ten minutes. Come along and see how it's done."

"Stand by those lines!" he bellowed to his seamen. "Smart, now! One fumble here and we're headed for Davy Jones' locker!"

Slade stood by the wheel as the little craft tacked along the coast. The wind had veered to the south and a few points west and she made slow going of it. Skipper Jack never took his eyes off the swirling water ahead, except from time to time to glance up at his sticks and the straining sails and shoot a swift glance shoreward. With uncanny skill he avoided the malevolent currents and the treacherous shoals. His booming voice bellowed orders that were instantly and skillfully obeyed. Once Slade ventured to ask why he did not stand farther offshore until the wreck was sighted. Skipper Jack jerked his head towards the hills in and beyond the marsh.

"Strange jiggers snoop around up there, waiting their chance," he said. "If we're offshore they can squat on some top with glasses and map our course. Then when we sidle in toward the wreck we might get a hot reception from somewhere among the rocks. In close this way, they'll have to come forward to get a sight of us and then we can sight them."

Slade nodded, appreciating Bowen's canniness.

Many hours passed before they sighted the wreck. The Santa Rosa, or rather the battered hulk that had once been the Santa Rosa, straddled a shiny reef. With little more than a stiff breeze blowing at the moment, the waves did not break across her deck, although the surf frothed and pounded about her sides.

"Couple more days, though, even if it doesn't come a hard blow, and she'll break up," said Bowen.

As they neared the wreck, Slade studied the sea. He saw that here and there were channels of deep and clear water with the surf pounding and spurting on either side: channels that led in to the shore, which a boat, skillfully handled, could negotiate even in time of storm.

Clear on the air came the mournful toll of the bell buoy, which dipped and bobbed some distance out to sea from the shoal and not more than half a mile east of where the wreck lay. And as they drew opposite the buoy, Slade saw that one of the deep, still channels of clear water ran straight from the buoy to the shore. No

136

wonder the wreckers had had no difficulty silencing its warning voice.

Skipper Jack nodded toward the buoy. "Why the devil the lubbers didn't hear that plain warning of shoal ahead is beyond me," he growled. "You can hear that big clapper a mile before you come to it, even with the wind blowing great guns. They must have been deaf, or drunk, which is more likely."

He studied the wreck with narrowed eyes, nodded his shaggy head. "We can do it," he announced. "Boats can make it to her all right."

Opposite the wreck but well out from the dangerous shoal, Bowen brought her about and the Isabella hung in the wind. Two boats were lowered and Slade, Sheriff Barkley, Lafe Secrets, the express company president, the two deputies, several cattlemen, who completed the sheriff's posse, and Skipper Jack ran up alongside the Santa Rosa and clambered aboard.

Bulwarks, deck-house galley, cabin skylight and the wheel had gone over the side. The masts had snapped off close to the deck. There was water in the hold.

There was no water in the captain's cabin, but there was plenty of evidence of recent violence and grim tragedy aboard the doomed vessel. The door of a big iron safe bolted to the forward bulkhead lay on the floor of the cabin. It had been wrenched or blown from its hinges. The safe was empty.

Beside the battered door lay two dead men. One wore a uniform adorned with brass buttons and much gold braid. He was a swarthy man with lank black hair now rimmed with sea salt. His ill-fated companion was dressed in a less ornate uniform. Both men had been shot.

"The Mexican captain and his mate," said Lafe Secrets. "In my opinion it is a plain case of mutiny and robbery. The crew mutinied, murdered the captain and first officer and stole the gold from the safe and put off in one of the ship's boats. Of course, the ship went on the rocks, with nobody to handle her. The warning bell buoy meant nothing. I would say they headed back to Mexico. Sheriff, you'd better get word there as quickly as possible. Perhaps the *rurales* will be able to run them down."

Horton, the express company president, and the cattlemen nodded agreement. Sheriff Barkley also nodded but did not otherwise comment. Captain Jack glanced at Slade with puckered eyes and shook his head slightly. El Halcon inclined his own head the merest trifle.

While the others examined the manifest and the log, which they unearthed in the cabin, Slade and Captain Jack walked about the deck.

"Secrets may be right, it could be mutiny and robbery, but to my mind it don't make sense," Bowen said in low tones. "Why would the crew abandon ship and take to an open boat with a storm coming on, when they had a tight little ship in their hands? Answer me that one, will you? If they figured on running ashore someplace with the gold they'd know they could make better time with less chance of getting overhauled by using the ship. Something mighty, mighty funny about all this, son."

"I'm ready to agree with you," Slade replied. Abruptly he let the full force of his level gray eyes rest on the mariner's face.

"Captain Jack," he said softly, "will you do me a favor?"

"Anything I can, son," Bowen instantly responded. "What is it?"

"Don't tell anybody else what you just told me."

Skipper Jack stared, then nodded. "Okay, son, if you want it that way," he promised. "Reckon you've got a reason for asking."

"Yes, I have a reason," Slade replied. "Thank you, Captain. Jack."

It was swiftly growing dark beneath a cloudy sky when the Isabella got under way again for the return trip. The wind had veered into the southwest. Skipper Jack was at the wheel. Sheriff Barkley, not feeling too good on the rough sea, was in the cabin lying down. The others were scattered about, some topside, some down below. Walt Slade, his black head bared to the lash of the wind, leaned on the taffrail, watching the phosphorescence of the wake as the Isabella heeled over before the breeze. A mist was swirling up from the water and the night was already black. Slade was occupied with his own thoughts and paid little attention to what went on around him. He turned his head at a slight, stealthy sound.

And at that instant, hands like bands of steel seized him from behind. Before he could offer resistance he was swung off his feet and sent hurtling over the rail. He hit the black water with a sullen plunge and vanished beneath the roily surface. The Isabella swept on through the misty night.

CHAPTER
FIFTEEN

The lights of the sloop were but a faint glimmer in the mist when Slade broke surface. He shouted once, then saved his breath to battle the swirling currents that instantly gripped him. He had just time to gasp a quick breath before he went under again. He fought desperately to regain the surface but his guns and his sodden clothing dragged him down. His lungs were bursting when at length he got his head above water once more. With all his iron strength he battled the deadly drag of the current that threatened to sweep him out to sea. By a mighty effort he managed to keep his head above water. He could hear the muffled roaring of the breakers on the rocks and he knew that once he was fairly in the wild surf he would quickly be battered to pieces. And to be swept out to sea would also be fatal.

He grazed a fang of stone, struck sideways against another and went sick and dizzy with the shock. The air was full of spray and he breathed as much salt water as oxygen. Choking and gasping he went under. His chest felt as if an iron band was slowly crushing his ribs together. Red flashes stormed before his eyes, flashes that changed to an opal-tinted mist. It had been bad enough when the drygulcher's bullet knocked him into the bay beside the Gallo Rojo, but this was infinitely worse. Here was no still water agitated only by the inward sweeping waves, this maelstrom of swirling currents and eddies.

It was his study of the currents and channels earlier in the day that saved him. His eardrums were splitting from the clang and thunder of the buoy bell close at hand. With all his remaining strength he swam straight for the buoy. Now he was directly opposite it, and a mighty current seized him and swept him with it at frightening speed.

Slade did not try to battle the current, for it was running smooth and straight. He merely fought to keep his head above water. On it swept him, between the grinning teeth of two reefs that showered him with spray. Now he was past their deadly menace and hurtling shoreward. A few more minutes and suddenly his knees and his hands touched firm, smooth sand. He floundered erect and was instantly knocked down by the rush of the water. This time he crawled and scuttled forward, holding his breath, striving against the fierce undertow that threatened to hurl him back to destruction. His head broke surface as a receding wave washed over his back, tearing at his body with tenacious liquid fingers.

Again he got to his feet, and now the water came barely to his knees. He sloshed through the thinning foam, staggered drunkenly, took a couple more groping steps and fell limply on the pebbly surface of a stretch of beach.

142

"Three times in the water since I hit this infernal section!" he gulped aloud as he strove to get some air back into his lungs. "I'm afraid to take my boots off for fear I'll find I'm getting web-footed! I trust this *is* the last time."

The cold bite of the night air through his wet clothing finally aroused Slade from the coma of intense fatigue. Stiffly he got to his feet, his teeth chattering, and with uncertain steps climbed the beach until he reached the trail which ran not far from the water's edge. He paused a moment to get his bearings, peering at obstacles dimly outlined in the wan starlight that seeped through the mist. He turned east, knowing that less than a quarter of a mile distant was the chimney rock which had given him shelter the night of the storm. The stiffness left his limbs as he trudged along the track, his blood circulated more freely and he suffered less from cold.

Just the same he was profoundly thankful when the dark loom of the rock showed directly ahead. He reached it, broke off an armful of twigs and branches from the nearby growth and groped his way into the hollow formed by the overhang and the fallen talus. His bottle of matches was unbroken and he soon got a fire going which he fed to a roaring blaze. Removing his clothing he held the garments to the fire until the heat had dried them somewhat. They were still damp when he donned them but the fire would soon take care of that. He built up the fire some more, placed a store of fuel close to hand and stretched out on the ground.

Almost instantly he was sleeping the sleep of sheer exhaustion.

The east was brightening with wan light when Slade awoke. The fire had died down to a smolder but he quickly revived it with more fuel and hunkered over it until he was warm again. His clothes had dried while he was asleep and though stiff and sore and bruised in a multitude of places he felt very much himself again. As the light strengthened he set out on the long and weary trudge to town. Now, however, he could take a much more direct route than the circuitous track he was forced to follow when he rode away from the old house in the swamp.

The sun had flamed down behind the western hills. The windows of Palma were changing from pale, vacantly-staring eyes to golden squares and rectangles. In the sheriff's office, Sheriff Jake Barkley and Skipper Jack Bowen conversed gloomily. The sheriff's face was lined and haggard. Skipper Jack's brow was black as a thundercloud.

"Oh, he went over the side, all right," he was saying. "No doubt about that. We searched that blasted ship from jib to taffrail, topside and below, and all we found was his hat. Blast it, anyhow! I either take to folks first off or I don't take to 'em at all, and I took to that young feller amazing. What I can't understand is how he come to go over the rail. He wasn't no lubber that would get pitched when she heeled."

"He might have been helped over," growled the sheriff.

144

"Maybe," conceded Skipper Jack, "but by who?"

"If I knew who, I'd help him over the side — into eternity!" Sheriff Barkley declared grimly. "Wonder if there was any chance he might have swum ashore, if he was alive when he went over?"

"Mighty little chance, I'd say," Bowen replied morosely. "In that mess of currents and eddies nobody could last —"

Suddenly his voice died, his jaw sagged and he stared unbelievingly toward the door.

A man had just entered, a tall man whose clothes were dusty and wrinkled and whose face was lined with fatigue. But his black-lashed gray eyes were a-dance with little laughing lights and his pose was vigorous and alert.

Skipper Jack went across the room in two great bounds. He seized Walt Slade by the shoulders in a grip of iron and shook him till his teeth rattled.

"Son!" he roared joyously in a voice that quivered the rafters, "how in the devil did you do it?"

Skipper Jack forced Slade into a chair. "You look plumb tuckered," he declared. "Don't say a word till I get back. I'm steering for a restaurant with all sails drawing, to get you hot coffee and something to eat."

Slade sat down gratefully. He was feeling a bit tuckered. Sheriff Barkley reached over and patted his shoulder and deftly manufactured a cigarette which he handed to him.

"I've a notion you can stand a drag," he said as he held a match to the tip. "I got a bottle in the drawer if you'd care for a snort."

"I think I'll have the coffee first," Slade decided as he drew deep on the brain tablet, after which they smoked in silence till Captain Jack reappeared with the food.

As he ate, Slade told them what had happened.

"And you didn't get a look at the sidewinder?" the sheriff asked.

Slade shook his head. "It was pitch dark and all over in a flash," he explained. "About all I can say is that he was big and tall and strong as the devil."

"Describes several of my swabs," growled Captain Jack, adding, "but I've known them all for a long time and I'm hanged if I can see any of them going in for murder."

"Doubtful if any of them would," Slade agreed.

"Then who?" demanded the sheriff.

"That," Slade replied, "remains to be found out."

"Everybody will be glad to hear you turned up," said the sheriff. "They all felt bad about it. Lafe Secrets especially. He'll sure be surprised when he sees you."

"I expect he will be," Slade agreed dryly.

"I'll tell him you're okay when I drop in at the Dollar Down a little later," the sheriff promised. "Now I suppose you're going to bed?"

"You're darn right I am," Slade replied heartily. "I feel like I could sleep for a week, but I guess I'll compromise on morning."

"Drop in tomorrow," said Barkley. "There's a big shipment coming along from the railroad about noon. Two hundred thousand dollars in gold coin consigned to the Amalgamated people at Tuxpan, for payrolls and purchases. They're taking no chances on that one.

146

There'll be about a dozen armed guards along. Just the same I won't feel right till it's locked safe in the bank vault. I'll feel even better when it's on a ship a couple of days later. They can't hold me responsible for anything that might happen on the high seas. By the way, here's your hat. We saved it just in case you might need it."

Saying good night to Barkley and Skipper Jack, Slade left the office. He did not enter the Gallo Rojo but, after making sure Shadow was okay, headed straight for his room and bed.

Mid-morning of the next day found him in the sheriff's office.

"I told Secrets you were all right," the sheriff remarked. "He was surprised, and 'peared pleased. Said to tell you he was mighty glad nothing bad happened to you and seemed mighty puzzled over how such a thing could have happened. Seemed to think somebody of Skipper Jack's crew must have had a grudge against you for some reason or other. Reckon there are folks who do sort of hold a grudge against El Halcon."

"Quite probably," Slade conceded. "Secrets around today?"

Barkley shook his head. "Rode up to his ranch last night," he replied. "Said he'd been neglecting the spread and with roundup time coming along he figured to spend a few days there getting ready."

Slade nodded, his eyes thoughtful.

The treasure wagon arrived shortly before noon. Slade and the sheriff watched the stout canvas sacks carried into the bank under the eyes of vigilant guards and stored in the vault.

Slade didn't think much of the vault, which was really nothing more than a big old-fashioned iron safe. However, it would offer considerable resistance to an attempt to batter it open, which would take time.

After seeing the gold placed under lock and key, Slade strolled along the waterfront alone and thinking deeply. He had plenty to think about.

Slade was at last convinced that he knew his man. The try at drowning him in the waters of Resaca Bay was the clincher.

Lafe Secrets was the guiding genius of the outlaw band known as the Night Riders — Lafe Secrets, of vague antecedents. Nobody seemed to know just where he had come from or what he had been before he showed up in Palma a few years before. He had adroitly delayed Sheriff Barkley's pursuit of the stage robbers and at the forks of the trail subtly induced the sheriff to take the wrong turn. He was in a position to obtain information relative to valuable shipments by sea or rail. He had deliberately lied when he told Sheriff Barkley that he had spent the day on his range and that he and his hands had gone to bed early the night Slade saw him and his bunch riding in long after midnight. Lafe Secrets was the boss who avoided Slade's bullets by dodging back among his men when Slade fought a running fight with the outlaws after escaping from the old marsh house.

All of which was fine, but just the same he did not have a scintilla of proof against Secrets. And Slade experienced an uneasy premonition that Secrets, finding the section getting a bit too hot for him and El

Halcon hard on his trail, was planning to pull out. And if he did, there wasn't a thing Slade could do about it. Secrets could openly wind up his business affairs and ride away in broad daylight, and Slade would have to stand by idly and watch him go.

Well, maybe the varmint would do something to tip his hand, but Slade had another unpleasant feeling that it would be done in a way hard to combat. Secrets always appeared to be one jump ahead of him. While he had been concentrating on rather stupid, bumbling Clark Waters and Mexican Pete, Secrets had been rolling merrily along, robbing and murdering and filling his poke. The hellion was a shrewd article. But his action when he, Slade, was throwing lead at him outside the marsh house hinted at one flaw that might make him vulnerable. Secrets might have a little paper in his backbone and an undue regard for his own personal safety.

That night Slade again visited the rear corner of the Gallo Rojo building, via the cracks-between-the-timbers route. Peering around he could see the wan glow coming out the windows and could faintly hear a murmur of voices. He made his way back to his own window chuckling. Mexican Pete's "contraband" was still in the back room. Quite likely his ride up to Carlson, the railroad town, was to make arrangements for disposing of it. Although it was not exactly the thing for a peace officer to do, Slade wished him luck in the venture. Pete might be busting the law a bit but nevertheless Slade felt he could be doing the country and the state a good turn in the long run. Sometimes

149

laws passed at the instigation of a particular section can work a not-intended hardship in others.

Slade got a good night's rest and aside from a few bruises was little the worse for his hazardous adventure in Resaca Bay. After a hearty breakfast, he repaired to Sheriff Barkley's office to learn if anything had developed during the night.

There hadn't, but there would soon.

Slade had been with the sheriff less than half an hour when a cowhand rode a lathered horse into town.

"The sheriff!" he bawled to people on the street. "Where'll I find the sheriff?"

He was directed to Barkley's office and a moment later leaped from his horse while it was still in motion, dropped the split reins to the ground and pounded into the office.

"The Rafter K!" he sputtered. "Herd widelooped — two night hawks killed — 'nother got busted shoulder!"

"Hold it, son! Hold it!" said Sheriff Barkley. "Calm down and tell us what you're talking about."

"The Rafter K," the cowboy repeated, "a bunch of hellions swooped down on the shipping herd just before daylight. Shot up the night hawks and hightailed with the cows. They figured they'd killed Pat, too, I reckon, but he come to and made it to the house. Roused out the boys and we all skalleyhooted after the sidewinders. Caught up with 'em. The boys figure they've got 'em trapped in Manzanita Canyon, but there's nearly twenty of the devils and they need help to root 'em out.

150

Jackson, you know, the boss, sent me to town to get you."

"Who got killed?" asked the sheriff.

The cowboy rattled off a couple of names. The sheriff nodded.

"Two of Jackson's best hands," he observed grimly. "I ain't seen you before, have I, son?"

"Reckon not," the puncher agreed. "Ain't never been in no trouble and I signed up with Jackson just a couple of weeks back. Say, does this sort of thing happen often down here? I'm beginning to think I'd better stayed in the Trinity country. I just missed being picked for the graveyard shift last night. I'd have got it, too."

"Chances are you would have," conceded the sheriff. "Okay, I'll get a bunch together and hustle up there. How many did you say there were of the devils?"

"Close to twenty, I'd say," replied the cowboy. "I'm going over and get a snort. I need it."

The puncher left the office. Sheriff Barkley turned to Slade. "Manzanita Canyon is a box," he said. "If Jackson and his hands have got 'em herded in there, they should be able to hold 'em till we get there. The Rafter K is a big outfit, biggest in the section, and works twenty-five or thirty hands. They've had trouble before — their west range runs into the hills. We'll need a dozen men or more. Hustle over to the Dollar Down, will you? I think you'll find my deputies there having something to eat. Tell them to get busy while I round up some folks. We'll get going as fast as we can. The Rafter K bunch are plenty salty, but like most cowhands, they're bum shots. If the hellions decide to

151

come out in a rush, they're liable to make a getaway, or some of them."

Twenty minutes later the posse, fifteen strong, including Slade and the sheriff, headed north at a fast clip. They hadn't gone far when Slade, who had been studying the faces of his companions, turned to the sheriff. "Where's that hand who brought the word?" he asked. "I don't see him."

"Reckon that snort he went after growed to a flock," grunted Barkley. "That's usually the way. We don't need him, to heck with him. Speed up, boys, we've got nigh to twenty miles to cover."

CHAPTER
SIXTEEN

Less than an hour after the posse set out, a second rider stormed into town, a swarthy, hard-faced man who spurred a foaming horse down the main street. He yelled like a Comanche as he rode and seemed wildly drunk with excitement. In front of the Dollar Down saloon he jerked his horse to a skittering stop and rolled from the saddle, waving a buckskin sack over his head.

"Gold!" he bawled. "Millions of it! Acres of it! The biggest strike ever! Millions!"

Still yelling, he dashed into the saloon, scattering the sparse early gathering at the bar.

Not for long was the gathering sparse. Attracted by the uproar, men came running from all directions — shopkeepers in aprons, clerks in shirt sleeves.

"Drinks!" howled the author of the excitement. "Drinks for the house! Belly up, gents, belly up! Drinks for everybody!"

He up-ended the sack and poured a stream of rock fragments and dully glowing lumps onto the bar.

"Gold!" he bellowed. "Gentlemen, come and get it!"

"Where'd you get it? Where'd it come from? Good gosh, look at those nuggets!" were the lucid peaks above the cloud of incoherent bawling.

"Back in the hills to the southwest of here, down toward the marshes," came the answer. "Whole ledges and out-croppings. I'll show you. I staked my claim and aim to file my notices. There's plenty for everybody. Drink up, gents! I'll be back in a minute — don't want anybody to lose out!"

But the crowd had not intention of losing him. They streamed after him, gathering new recruits by the second, toward the waterfront and the Gallo Rojo. The Dollar Down bartender shucked off his apron, leaped over the bar and headed the procession.

At the Gallo Rojo the performance was repeated. The wild-eyed miner gulped whiskey, ordered food and consumed it and demanded drinks for everybody. He flung a plump sack over the bar in payment.

"To hell with the change!" he whooped as more nuggets cascaded into view. "I'm heading to the courthouse to file my claim. Get ready, gents, I'm riding back to the hills in an hour."

There is something about raw gold that sets men's blood on fire. No amount of gold coin could have such an effect; but the stark, elemental reality of nuggets and dust gleaned from the stubborn earth quickens the pulses, destroys judgment and brings out all that is reckless and adventurous. At the courthouse, the agitated clerk could hardly fill out the necessary forms, and when the task was completed, he flung down his pen and followed the miner out the door, his companion employees crowding after him.

Far and wide flew the news, to every building in the little town — and the rush was on!

The posse did not spare their horses during the ride north to the Rafter K ranchhouse and Manzanita Canyon only a few miles beyond. The embattled Rafter K cowhands might be hard put to hold the outlaws at bay.

"They may be waiting for dark, but they're liable to bust loose at any time," predicted the sheriff.

Slade nodded agreement. He was in an exultant mood. Looked like the break he'd hoped for was at hand. Secrets, nervous and apprehensive, had apparently tried for a last big haul before pulling out. Slade gathered that the Rafter K shipping herd was a large one and at the current prices of even widelooped cows would run into plenty of money.

Their horses were sweating when they sighted the Rafter K ranchhouse that stood close to the trail. As they drew near they could make out the figure of a man sitting in a chair on the veranda, his boots propped comfortably on the porch railing.

"Why, it's Berne Jackson himself!" exclaimed the sheriff. "Looks like it's all over and they don't need our help."

The sheriff's voice was jubilant, but Walt Slade's expression was serious. To him the ranchowner did not look like a man who had suffered the loss of two of his men and had just been through a brush with desperate owl-hoots.

As they foamed up to the ranchhouse, Jackson shouted a surprised greeting.

155

"What the dickens you doing way up here, Jake, and in such a hurry?" he wanted to know.

"What am I doing here? You sent for me, didn't you?" bawled the sheriff.

"Heck, no I didn't send for you, you spavined old coot," retorted Jackson. "I'm particular about the company I keep. Say, have you fellers all been eatin' loco weed? What's this all about, anyhow?"

The sheriff told him, the explanation embellished with vivid profanity. Jackson shook his head in bewilderment.

"I ain't lost any cows, ain't had anybody killed and ain't hired a new hand for months," he declared. "Jake, somebody's been bamboozelin' you!"

The sheriff started another tirade, directed at the pseudo Rafter K hand who had brought the phony message to town, but Slade stopped him before he got in full stride.

"Listen, Barkley," he said, "there's something mighty funny about this, and I don't like the looks of it. Seems somebody was mighty anxious to get you out of town, and quite a few of the town's able-bodied men along with you. Looks to me like somebody is all set to pull something somewhere else."

"You mean that gold in the vault?" Barkley instantly asked.

"I don't know," Slade admitted. "That doesn't seem to make sense — there are still plenty of men in town to take care of an attack on the bank, but just the same it looks bad. Now I'll tell you what. My horse is still in good shape. He can take a lot more than most. I'm

156

heading back to town as fast as he can take me there. You and the rest of the boys water your critters and rub them down and give them half an hour's rest. Then hightail after me."

"But you'll be taking a chance if something is going on in town or somewhere around, going it by yourself," protested the sheriff. "You'd better wait for the rest of us."

"I'll risk it," Slade said tersely. "Maybe by getting there in a hurry I can prevent something bad happening. Be seeing you!"

He turned Shadow and set out on the back-track at a moderate pace, gradually lengthening the black's stride as he got underway.

As he rode, Slade wracked his brains to try and figure what the outlaws might have in mind. It seemed arrant nonsense to think they intended to stage a raid on the bank. Before they could hope to batter open the vault or force the bank officials to open it, there would be a hullabaloo that would arouse the town. And, as he told Sheriff Barkley, there were still plenty of men in town to take care of them if it came to a fight. So he thought.

Well, there was no use wasting his energy on conjecture. When he got to Palma he would very likely learn the truth. He estimated that Barkley and the posse would be something more than an hour behind him at the very least. Plenty could happen in an hour. He settled himself in the saddle and sent Shadow forward at a fast and steady pace. The great horse was still in excellent condition and the miles flowed swiftly under his speeding hoofs.

When Slade reached Palma, slightly before mid-afternoon, he rode into what was apparently a deserted settlement. Nearly all the shops were closed and locked, and most of the saloons, including the Dollar Down. Houses had an empty look. The old bank president stood in the doorway of the bank building, the sunlight glinting on his silvery hair, and talked animatedly with another oldster who leaned on a cane and cupped his hand to a dulled ear. A few woman gazed out the windows. Children played in the street. Slade's jaw tightened, his face was bleak. Something was very much wrong.

He pulled up in front of the Dollar Down. An elderly bartender, one of the night-shift men, lounged against the wall.

"What happened, where is everybody?" Slade demanded.

"Gold strike back in the hills, the biggest ever," the drink juggler replied in mournful tones. "Don't reckon you'll find an able-bodied man in town. I'd be gone too if it wasn't for this game leg of mine. I can hardly walk, much less ride, drat the luck!"

Slade dragged the details of the story from him. Then he rode to the Gallo Rojo. He found Mexican Pete sitting alone at the bar, smoking a cigar.

"Nobody left but me," he said with a wry smile.

"Why didn't you join the stampede?" Slade asked.

"I have other business to attend to," Pete replied quietly.

Slade nodded as if he understood. "Strike really as rich as they say it is?" he asked.

For answer Pete took a sack from the till and spilled the contents on the bar.

"See for yourself," he said.

Slade stared curiously at the yellowish lumps and the metal clinging to the rock fragments which formed part of the contents of the sack.

"Not placer stuff — fragments chipped from a ledge," he remarked, bending closer. He picked up one of the fragments and examined it with the eye of a geologist, turning it over in his slim fingers. He raised his gaze to Mexican Pete's face.

"Pete," he asked, "do you know anything about mining?"

Mexican Pete shook his head. "Nothing," he replied. "Why? Isn't the gold good?"

"None better," Slade answered, "but this is the first time in my experience that I ever saw gold mixed up with granite fragments!"

"I do not understand," Mexican Pete said in bewildered tones.

"I don't, either," Slade agreed with grim irony. "It's like this, gold is never found in paying quantities in granite ledges, only in quartz or allied rock, but here we have gold clinging to granite fragments. Why in blazes didn't somebody notice it? Aren't there any old mining men in this town?"

"I have heard the *Señor* Secrets is familiar with mines. Others? Perhaps, of that I know not. People see what they wish to see," he philosophized shrewdly.

"Men burning with the gold fever are apt to see gold only."

Slade nodded. "Exactly," he said. "There's no doubt but a ledge was salted. Salted with melted gold coins, I'd say. They poured the molten metal over and among the rock fragments. Looks good, all right. The only slip they made was in not hunting up quartz fragments instead of using granite that was ready to hand. Guess they figured nobody would notice, anyhow, 'seeing' gold, as you said. Looks like a crazy trick, doesn't it? Yes, crazy like a fox! Pete, I'm taking a little ride up the trail. I want you to promise me you'll stay right here until I get back."

"Assuredly, if you ask," was the wondering reply, "but why?"

"Tell you when I get back — and the chances are there'll be no need to tell, if things turn out the way I figure they will," Slade answered cryptically as he headed for the door.

His face wearing a bewildered expression, Mexican Pete watched him ride swiftly toward the hill trail. Then, shaking his head, he hurried to the back room door, unlocked it and passed through, carefully locking it behind him.

Slade did not ride far, only to where he could see the creast of a rise some three miles distant. He pulled up and sat watching the distant hilltop. For some minutes he sat motionless, then suddenly he leaned forward in the saddle.

160

Over the crest was flowing a number of black dots. Slade quickly identified them as nearly twenty horsemen.

"Thought so," he muttered. "It's them, all right." He turned Shadow and rode swiftly back to Palma's main street. He drew a gun and fired three evenly-spaced shots in the air, the danger warning or call for help of cattle country. He waited a moment, then fired three more shots. He pulled Shadow to a halt, dismounted and waited. Drawing the star of the Rangers from its pocket he pinned it to his shirt front.

In answer to the fusillade, several old men came hobbling up. A moment later they were joined by the old bank president, the crippled bartender and the fat little manager of the express company.

"What's wrong, feller?" the barkeep called anxiously, staring at the star on Slade's breast.

"The Night Riders are headed this way, coming fast," Slade told them. "They aim to clean the bank after staging the fake gold strike to get folks out of town. There's liable to be a pitched battle fought in the streets before this is finished. Hustle through the town and collect the women and children and everybody else. There's no telling what these murdering devils will do if they get control of the town. Head everybody for the waterfront. There are a couple of big lighters tied up at the quay. Load onto them and shove out into the bay. Get way out — beyond rifle range. You'll be safe there. That's what the folks of Linnville did when the Comanches raided the town and burned it back in Ben McCulloch's time."

161

The bank president wrung his hands. "Two hundred thousand dollars in gold in the bank!" he quavered.

"And that's nearly eight hundred pounds of metal," Slade told him. "You can't carry that on your back. Move, all of you, and do as I told you."

They moved, the bank president still wringing his hands but his lined face wearing a determined look.

"We'll do our part, Ranger!" shouted the crippled barkeep, hobbling along as fast as he could. "Good hunting! We ain't got nothing to worry about with a Ranger on the job."

Slade appreciated the compliment and hoped it wouldn't be misplaced. He mounted Shadow and rode to the Gallo Rojo. He found Mexican Pete standing in the doorway, a rifle in his hands.

"I heard what was said," Pete remarked calmly, staring at the Ranger star, his gaze a bit apprehensive.

"Come inside," Slade told him. Shadow, at a word from his master, obediently trotted for the stable across the way, the door of which stood open.

Inside the *cantina*, Slade held Mexican Pete with his steady gaze. "Pete, he said quietly," you have been and are violating the laws of your country and your state. Yes, I know, smuggling Chinese across the Border isn't looked on by most folks as a very ornery chore. Personally, I can't say as I blame the poor devils for wanting to get into a decent country to live, and so far as I've been able to notice, Chinese most always make good citizens. One of the best friends I ever had was our old Chinese cook who died fighting with his last breath when wide-loopers raided our spread. Now

162

listen — "You have at least a dozen Chinese holed up in that big back room. Chinese are good fighters. You have rifles and sixguns, yes? Break them out, arm the Chinese and we'll stand those hellions. off till the folks all get in the clear. No telling what those murdering devils might do. And perhaps we can stand them off till the sheriff and his bunch get here and save the money in the bank. Hustle — they'll be showing any minute now."

"But how will I tell the Chinese what is expected of them?" protested Pete. "I do not speak their tongue and my man who knew a few words deserted with the stampede."

"I can sling it a bit," Slade answered. "The old cook taught me a good deal and perhaps I can remember enough to put it across. I'll try."

Pete flung the door wide, hurried across a dimly lighted room to a second door which he unlocked and opened. Slade stepped forward and gazed into the startled yellow faces of the occupants of the big room. He held up his hand to still a rising murmur and spoke to them, slowly, carefully, trying to recall the all but forgotten, syllables.

"Men," he said in effect, "you want to enter America, to become Americans. The first privilege of a good American is to fight for his country and its laws. Now is your chance to fight."

A big Manchu with a pockmarked face and an enormous spread of shoulders, who had been lending an attentive ear, stepped forward.

"Me speak," he said in English. "You tell over. Me speak them."

Slade repeated what he had said, in English. The Manchu turned and let loose a string of something that sounded like firecrackers exploding in a barrel. His fellows crowded toward him, chattering gaily. The Manchu added something that Slade could not understand but which he gathered from the tonal inflection to be a complicated curse. He turned to the Ranger.

"They fight," he said laconically.

CHAPTER
SEVENTEEN

Mexican Pete began taking rifles and revolvers from a cabinet and handed them to Slade who passed them out to the Chinese. The Manchu, who was evidently familiar with arms, was rapidly explaining the mechanism of the Winchesters and Colts.

Clutching their weapons and blinking in the sudden light, the yellow men followed Slade and Mexican Pete into the street.

"Not a minute too soon, either," Slade muttered as a faint murmur which he recognized as the drumming of fast hoofs sounded from the west. He glanced at the loaded lighters, which were still too close to the shore, within easy rifle range.

"To Main Street," he ordered. "They'll turn in there, and we'll try and make things interesting for them. Tell the boys to hold their fire until I give the word," he directed the Manchu. "I'm a peace officer and have to conduct myself as one."

They raced up a convenient alley and reached the main street. It was silent and deserted, but the pound of hoofs was now clear and distinct.

"Spread out and line your guns with them," Slade said, an order which the Manchu relayed to his companions.

165

A moment later a compact body of horsemen bulged around the turn. They wore black masks and carried rifles. In the lead was a tall man swathed in a long black cloak. They jerked to a halt, staring at the bristle of gun barrels.

Walt Slade, a gun in each hand, stepped forward. His voice rang out, "In the name of the State of Texas! I arrest Lafe Secrets and others for robbery and murder! Anything you say —"

With a yell the tall leader flung up his rifle. Slade fired, left and right. The leader reeled sideways and pitched to the ground, his hat and black mask fluttered off to reveal Lafe Secrets' face.

That was enough for the Chinese. Screeching and whooping with excitement, they opened fire. With the exception of the Manchu they were execrable shots and even at that distance mostly managed to shoot over the heads of the horsemen. Nevertheless, four saddles were emptied at the first volley, while a fifth man reeled and dropped his rifle. For a moment the others milled in wild confusion, then with shouts of fury they drove their horses forward and fired with deadly aim.

Slade instantly realized how it must end now that the devils had gotten over their initial scare. Two of the Chinese were already dead and the broken arm of a third flapped against his side as he fired his rifle as best he could with one hand.

"Back to the Gallo Rojo!" Slade shouted. "We can hold them off there for a spell."

They darted down the alley, Slade and Mexican Pete covering the retreat. The Night Riders slowed up as they rounded the corner. More empty saddles showed in their ranks and they hesitated to face those two unerring guns.

Another Chinese was down before they reached the waterfront and blood streamed from a flesh wound Slade had received in his right shoulder. The others dived through the swinging doors of the *cantina*.

"To the back room!" yelled Mexican Pete. "The door is strong and will delay them."

He snapped the lock when Slade, the last man, was through the door, and led the way to the big room which faced the bay. Heavy blows crashed and thundered on the outer barrier as he locked the second door.

"They're using tables for battering rams — it won't hold for long," Slade observed as he reloaded his Colts. The Chinese faced the inner door, their guns raised, prepared to sell their lives dearly. The hammering on the outer door increased.

Mexican Pete raised a trapdoor in the floor. A dark opening yawned. Slade caught a glimpse of a steep descent something like a grain chute.

"There is an opening at the bottom which leads to the water," Pete said. "Send the Chinese down quickly. The opening is narrow — just room for one man to slip through at a time."

"Those devils will pick them off in the water like ducks," Slade objected.

"I have a card yet to play," Mexican Pete said coolly as the outer door fell with a rending crash. He turned to the side wall and loosened a narrow panel. From the opening disclosed he drew a snaky looking fuse.

"The place is mined — dynamite planted above the piles," he explained as he struck a match and touched it to the fuse. "I expected to have to leave here hurriedly some time. I have enemies, many among those outside the door, with whom I refused to work. Hurry, the fuse is quick burning and short."

Slade hustled the Chinese through the door, one at a time. The black heads vanished from view into the darkness. The sound of splashes drifted upward. Mexican Pete stood beside him, his eyes on the shortening fuse that gave off wisps of smoke and spurts of glittering sparks. The door creaked and groaned as blows were showered upon it.

The last Chinese vanished from sight, the last splash sounded.

"You next, *amigo!*" said Mexican Pete.

Slade stepped back. "You first," he answered.

Mexican Pete's mocking, silvery laugh rang out. He seized Slade about the waist and slung him into the opening.

The Ranger shot down the steep slant, bumping over the cleats that had provided handholds for men climbing up from the boats, unable to halt his progress. He reached the opening at the bottom of the chute. His legs slipped through but his big shoulders stuck. With a desperate effort he freed himself and dropped. Just as he vanished beneath the surface the world above exploded in flame and roaring sound."

168

Half stunned by the terrific concusion, Slade dived deep as he could, fighting frantically to stay submerged as once before in these very waters he had striven to gain the surface. All about were prodigious splashes. Something huge and dark rushed past him. Another ponderous mass brushed his shoulder. He swam under water until his bursting lungs forced him to come up for air.

Floating timbers and other wreckage dotted the water. The sleek black heads of the Chinese bobbed toward the nearest lighter, which was splashing toward them.

Slade swam with easy strokes, despite the hampering weight of his clothes and guns. The sea was calm and there were no waves to battle. He lent a hand to the wounded Chinese who was making hard going of it with his single good arm. After a struggle they reached the lighter. Slade boosted the man aboard and then climbed to safety. Turning he gazed back at the mass of flaming wreckage that had been the Gallo Rojo and was the funeral pyre of Mexican Pete.

CHAPTER
EIGHTEEN

For long minutes Slade gazed, his eyes dark with pain. Then he bowed his black head for a moment, turned to the huddled occupants of the lighter and said in a matter-of-fact voice, "Guess you might as well row to shore, folks. Reckon the excitement is all over and you won't have to worry about the Night Riders any more."

By the time the lighters had docked, Sheriff Barkley and his posse galloped their foaming horses into town.

"We heard the blast and figured they'd blown up the bank," Barkley told Slade. "Just what did happen."

Slade told him. The sheriff shook his head in astonishment.

"So it was Secrets," he marvelled. "My God! I'd never have believed it."

"I didn't believe it for quite a while, either," Slade admitted. "He sure had me fooled and running around in circles."

"How the devil did you catch on to him?" the sheriff asked.

"Partly by a process of elimination," Slade explained. "It didn't take long to shove Clark Waters out of the picture. He just didn't fit at all. Pete, of course, was the logical suspect and he sure puzzled me for some time.

Secrets became really suspect when he told you he had been out all day on his range and that he and his hands had gone to bed early, when really he was down in the hills with his bunch, trying to drygulch me. Right then I knew there was something off-color about him, although of course I couldn't know that it was Secrets who'd engineered the deal to kill me. I just knew he wasn't right."

"Anything but right, evidently," conceded the sheriff.

"Then I managed to eliminate Pete," Slade continued, "when I found out that what he was doing and why the boats were slipping up to the Gallo Rojo in the middle of the night was just a little genteel chore of smuggling in Chinese. In fact, I'd already just about eliminated Pete as the head of the Night Riders."

"How's that, and when?" Barkley asked.

"When I had the rukus down by the old marsh house," Slade replied. "When the big hellion in the black cloak dodged back among his men as I was throwing lead at him. I knew Mexican Pete would never have done that. He'd have been right out in front blazing away for as long as he could pull trigger."

"You're darn right," growled Barkley. "He may have been tampering with the law a mite, but he was a man!"

Heads on all sides nodded grave agreement. Men crowded around to congratulate Slade and thank him for what he had done.

"I think a reward is due you, Ranger," declared the bank president. "I'm going to make it my business to see that you get one."

But Walt Slade smilingly shook his head. "Thanks, but I can't accept it," he said. "And I've a notion you can find a better use for the money."

The old president, gazing at the smoldering ruins of the Gallo Rojo, appeared struck by a sudden thought.

"If you won't accept it, I believe I have a good notion how it should be used," he said, and chuckled with pleasure.

"Come on over to my place and dry out," invited the sheriff. "Seems you spend more time in the water than out of it. Suppose you'll be riding back to the Post soon?"

"You're darn right!" Slade replied. "I'm going to rest up a day or two and then I'm heading into the desert where there isn't a drop of water. I never want to see another cupful!"

During the night and the following day, the angry, disgusted and disappointed goldseekers straggled back into town.

"The hellion led us to a ledge all right," one told the sheriff and Slade. "He washed out gold from the gravel at its base, and I reckon we all went plumb loco. A little later we couldn't find him when we looked for him. Of course, we still didn't suspect anything phony, but after washing more gravel and finding nothing and not being able to bust any color out of the rocks, we realized we'd been took, but we still couldn't understand why. I'd sure like to get my hands on that varmint."

"Go and root around in the water under what's left of the Gallo Rojo and maybe you'll find what's left of him." Slade suggested. "I figure he slipped away while

172

you were busy and notified his waiting bunch that everything was all set for the raid. The same goes for that supposed-to-be Rafter K cowhand who lured us out of town."

Some days later, Slade sat in Captain McNelty's office and regaled him with an account of what happened. The old Commander listened with great interest, chuckling from time to time as some humorous aspect of his lieutenant's misadventures struck him.

"Yes, everything ended up okay," Slade concluded, "only I spent so much time under water down there that I feel like I'm beginning to sprout fins!"

"The next chore I'm sending you on is in a mighty dry section," Captain Jim comforted him. "By the way, what became of the Chinese?"

Slade grinned. "Sort of lost track of them," he admitted, "but I heard that most of the spreads over to the north and west have all got Chinese cooks of late, and each owner is ready to swear that his is the prime picking of the lot."

Captain Jim chuckled creakily. "Full bellies go a long way toward making good citizens, and Chinese cooks are hard to beat," he allowed. "Reckon the law, especially Ranger law, can stretch a point now and then without cracking."

Slade nodded. He rose and walked to the open window and stood gazing into the southeast, his eyes brooding.

"What you thinking about, Walt?" Captain Jim asked.

Slade replied without turning around. "When I left down there, the folks in Palma were building a monument on the site of the Gallo Rojo," he said. "A simple shaft of granite, sort of tall, standing solid and four-square, ready to take on the wind and the sea, and anything else that comes its way. A fellow who is handy with a chisel had cut an inscription on the base. Not much, just a few words, *To The Memory of a Rather Good Man — PETE.*"

Betf 04.02.'Ben
21